Criminally Pieced Together

Book Three of the Fiber Mavens Mysteries

By

J. Traveler Pelton

copyright © 2020
Potpourri Publishing, Limited
Mt. Vernon, OH 43050

COPYRIGHT

Criminally Pieced Together: Book Three of the Fiber Mavens Mysteries by J. Traveler Pelton

Independently published by Potpourri Publishing
Cover design by RebecaCovers
Edited by Write Useful

Printed in the United States of America
First Edition published 2020
Books> fiction> mystery
ISBN: 9798648729476

Dedication

First, to my God and Creator, Savior and Guide, who gives us dreams and tasks, hammering our souls into shape as the blacksmith hammers metal into useful instruments. May we place ourselves in His forge and let Him work without interruption until what comes forth is pure gold.

I dedicate with love to all those who have been to the shadowy edge of life, looked over and decided to come back and try again. I've been there, I came back. May you keep the warmth and wealth of love in your hearts always. Love is what keeps us whole.

I dedicate it to my ancestors who walked the Red Road before me. Someday we will all walk the Skylands together. Until then our hearts beat with the drum of unity and peace.

May God grant us the courage to live with whatever life sends us and overcome it always with His peace.

Finally, to my readers, because a story isn't a story until someone else hears it; it is simply a phantasm, a dream in the maker's head. You make it live when you read it and for just a few brief moments, our imaginations combine and that's when magic is still alive...

Other Books by Traveler Pelton

Science Fiction

The First Oberllyn Family Trilogy: The Past
- The Oberllyn's Overland: 1855-1862
- Terrorists, Traitors and Spies 1900-1990
- Rebooting the Oberllyn's 2015-2020

The Second Oberllyn Family Trilogy: The Present
- The Infant Conspiracy
- Kai Dante's Stratagem
- The Obligation of Being Oberllyn

The Third Oberllyn Family Trilogy: The Future
- To Protect One's Own
- The Importance of Family Ties
- Kith and Kin, Together Again

The Fiber Mavens Mystery Series
- Quilting Can be Criminal
- Criminally Quilted
- Criminally Pieced Together

In Collaboration with T. Bear Pelton:
- Clan Falconer's War
- The Rise of the Rebellion
- Changeling's Clan
- Forged in Water and Fire

Family History
- Journey to Springhaven

Spiritual Works

- God Wanted to Write a Bestseller
- Big God, Little Me
- Lenten Stories for God's Little Children
- Natural Morning
- Ninety Days to The God Habit
- Tales for Advent and Christmas
- His Path Is Mine
- Calm Instead of Clamor
- Calming My Clamor

Other Authors Associated with Potpourri Publishing

Lynette Spencer of Write Useful
Sewing on a Budget
Vegetarian Cooking on a Budget

Dan Pelton
The Majestic Spectrum of God's Love

Chapter One

The plane landed without incident in Maui.

"That was an incredibly long flight!" declared Casey. "Where are we?"

"Glad you mom called to let us know they landed safely in Wisconsin," replied Brad. "We're in Hawaii on the island of Maui. I'm glad my buddy let us tag along on his flight. He runs freight from Ohio to here and it's only 8 hours using his plane. On a commercial flight, it takes twelve and right now, commercial I don't trust much."

"Hawaii? Really? I've always wanted to go!"

"Yes, we're staying in my friend's home and using it as a base to explore. We can take ferries to the other islands from Maui, and you're going to love how pretty it is. When my first wife died, I spent a month here getting over it. I like to never have come back, And I know you like to quilt and there is a quilt shop half a mile from our place. I signed you up for some afternoon quilt encounters. I'm going out ocean fishing. We're going snorkeling and shelling and hiking. Chuck's remote enough that it's private and close enough to ride a bike into the town. And there's a state park as well."

"And no hurting kids to rescue and no murder investigation and no FBI or homeland or anything for two whole weeks. I won't want to go home!" laughed his bride.

"Let's gather our stuff, we're stopped now," just as he said the words, the pilot's door opened on the tiny cabin and his friend Chuck came in, "Hey, guys, hope it didn't get too rough back there."

"Wasn't bad. Turbulence?" asked Brad as he picked up his carry-on.

"Yeah, don't mind it much, I always get some when we leave the continent and head out over the ocean. Did you see how pretty it was out today? Oh, and your bags are being unloaded. I gotta get down and get unloaded and fueled up. I'll drop you guys off on my way over to the post office and such."

"How long have you been doing this run?" asked Casey.

"Well, I'm a private contractor, and I have contracts with most the retailers, my biggest customer right now is Amazon, but the post office and fed ex ship overages with me, too. Got quite a load out there. Some of them come to pick their stuff up, the post office I take over to the main branch here. Then I'll come back, and eat something and get some shut-eye before I head out. I'll be back here in fifteen days; I have loads to the other islands over the next days so you won't see me much."

"I appreciate you bringing us stowaways," started Brad.

"Hey, No worries. Here come the stairs for us to get out."

The hull door popped open. Stairs attached to the side and they went down. Men were already unloading the cargo onto three or four carriers, Amazon's going directly into a truck, FedEx another truck, other couple packages going into smaller trucks, and the post office into a USPS truck.

"Hey, wife," called out Chuck. A pretty woman directing the unloading turned around, smiled and waved. She said something else to the package sorters, then came over dragging two suitcases.

"Safe flight, honey?" she asked, giving Chuck a quick kiss.

"Safe enough. Honey, you know Brad, but this is his new bride Casey. They're going to be in the beach house for a couple of weeks like I explained earlier."

"It was sort of sudden," explained Brad. "We were supposed to come over on American tomorrow but after the bomb at the airport, I saw Chuck's plane and decided to see if he had room since we were going to go to his place anyway. I hope we aren't inconveniencing you too much. My original plans included the San Diego zoo today, and flight out tomorrow."

"No, heavens no. I'm visiting my mom on the other side of the island for a few days. She has a bed and breakfast and her help went on vacation just as she booked a wedding party, so I'm going to help out. The house would be empty. I do it pretty often. Chuck and I will be leaving tonight after supper. When I get home, I'll show you around and it's all yours for two weeks. Then you puddle jump for home."

"I really appreciate the chance to do a safe trip. I am beginning not to trust anything." sighed Casey.

"You miss the leis this way." Remonstrated Candy. "they're part of the overall welcome to the island."

"Yeah, I'll need to get me some of those," replied Brad. "Do they come in Kevlar?" Chuck laughed and checked his load.

"Trucks almost full," replied Chuck. "Let me just make the maintenance arrangements and we'll be on our way."

Chuck trotted into the hanger, his wife completed the unloading and motioned them to get in Chuck's truck. Chuck came back and kissed his wife. She climbed into one truck to drive it off, another pilot came out to move Chuck's airplane for maintenance and refueling.

Chuck jumped into the truck beside Brad and grinned as he tossed flower leis around their necks. "There, you have officially been welcomed to Maui," he said. "Got those inside. They're jasmine, that's the smelly one, orchids and plumeria, leastwise, that's what the wife tells me. I like to garden but mostly fruit and veggies. I like nasturtiums. You can eat those."

"Always about food?" teased Brad.

"Hey, once you been in a POW camp, you get to appreciate grub in any form. Anyway, Candy is the flower person in the family." He backed the truck out of short term parking and headed out of the airport. "I'll just drop you off at the house. Candy left you some instructions on where stuff is, and you make yourself to home. We'll get there in about an hour and we can rustle up grub and get out of your way. You might want to walk on the beach. It's pretty. I think she got you some maps and stuff about the island to study and decide what you're going to do. They ought to be on your bed."

"I'm going fishing one day, and Casey's going to the quilt retreat in the afternoon."

"Really? She'll love Maude's place. Friendliest quilt shop in the state. Lots of island prints and her lessons are supposed to be outstanding."

"I can't wait," smiled Casey. "How did you and Candy and Brad all meet?"

"I'm brother to Brad's late wife and I was his best man at their wedding," answered Chuck who seemed to never slow down. Casey suspected he talked at over 100 words a minute with gusts of 150. "We met in the military, same unit, and then went to police academy together. Once we worked in the same police department but I took a bullet for the cause and retired here to open my delivery business. I met my Candy here at the airport. We've been happy together for nine years. No kids yet but that's going to change in about six months.

"Really?" exclaimed Brad. "Congratulations!"

"Yeah, I told Candy she needed to slow down and she told me when I did, she would. You guys are going to sleep in the nursery, which is really our guest room right now. I'm building onto the house another little extension to add a new guest room and bathroom, but it's not done. The little guy is due this fall around Thanksgiving. We are some excited. Anyway, the guest room opens onto the beach and you can just explore. We shouldn't be long."

"Thank you so much," began Casey when he took a breath.

"Oh, no worries. I'd have not made it through that POW camp if it hadn't been for Brad. He's been good to us. Here's our path," he turned off the road onto a side, single lane, long driveway through tall trees and bushes. Flowers appeared to be everywhere. He pulled up to a cottage just beyond the trees above the ocean.

"Candy calls it Floral Haven," he announced. "I just call it home. Let's get you inside and I have to tear off before the post office goes all barmy on me."

Floral Haven was a pastel, blue and cream, ranch-style home set back from the road, facing the ocean. It had a porch that surrounded it and French doors on the back. It sat up on seven-foot-high stilts. Underneath was a garage space. Climbing up, they had a wonderful view of the ocean and could just see the other islands. The sea color matched their home. It all blended as if it had grown together.

Inside, everything was in pastel colors, light greens and water sea aqua, the kitchen and living room flowing together with a dining bar between them. A huge, white, Persian cat lay across the back of the overstuffed couch and a large screen TV graced one wall. It smelled as if something was cooking in the oven, and Chuck went over and opened the front seaside doors to the ocean.

Following him, Casey and Brad walked out on the porch.

"It's beautiful," breathed Casey.

"Thank you. I like it meself," replied Chuck. "Now, there are drinks in the fridge and we'll be back soon. I put your suitcases in your room, so why not change into something more island-like and go for a walk on the beach? It's even prettier up close."

"That sounds divine after the long flight," she replied. Chuck left and they heard the truck pull out. Brad pulled her into his arms.

"See?" he murmured, "No close neighbors, a furry cat to pet, lovely beaches, and just look at her flower beds. As close to heaven without mountains as you can get."

After several minutes of uninterrupted kissing on the deck, Casey pulled back and smiled.

"Candy is probably almost here, so save that thought, but I need to go freshen up and taking a walk sounds wonderful."

"I agree. Let's go change and I hope you brought bikinis."

Chapter Two

Grandma stood up from the quilting frame.

"There! we've got it attached properly to the frame, and the batting and backing are baste layered right and tightened correctly and straight, and here are three spools of cotton thread and extra needles-always use cotton thread on a quilt, Annie, that polyester stuff cuts the fabric and will degrade the quilt after a while - let's see, coffee is set up to start at 2:30, and we have the tray of cookies ready. My old friends and your aunts are going to come and help us finish this. If we work hard, we can get it done to take home to your mom and Brad. Where's my binding strips? Oh yes, over here on the ironing board. Iron is off, good."

Annie wrinkled her nose. "It feels odd to think Brad's my dad now. I wonder how they're doing?"

"I'd be content knowing they got where ever it is safely." Her phone made a happy dance noise and she checked. "Well, that is the fastest I've ever had a prayer answered. This text is from your mom. She sent us a picture of the ocean-appears they're right on the beach and let's see, this one is a selfie of her and Brad walking by the waves. I think they're having a good time. My heavens! I didn't know your mom had a bikini!"

"She went into Columbus and bought them a couple of weeks ago and has been fretting about them ever since. Wish I was at the beach," said Annie. "Where is this?"

"She didn't say, just to let us know they got there safely. I'm going to send a selfie of us over here by the fireplace so she knows we got here safe too, and then let's go get some lunch."

"Good, I'm starving." With the selfie sent off through the ether, Grandma and Annie went into the kitchen to find her Grandmother's sister had left their lunches in the fridge on plates, green salad, tuna fish sandwiches, brownies, and fresh milk. The note she left suggested they set up the quilt and that Aunt Aria and Aunt Carolyn would be back by three, and if she wouldn't mind having the coffee started and the cookies out on platters, they could get right to the work. Grandma went over and set up the coffee and set it on a timer to start at 2:45.

After lunch, they decided to go outside and explore the local neighborhood. It was windy and they wore sweaters as they walked. Aunt Aria lived three blocks from downtown and the teen and grandma strolled happily past the houses, commenting to each other on how some of them looked like homes back in Lyonsville, with hanging baskets of flowers and well-kept yards. As they meandered down the sidewalks, they looked into the small shops that lined two blocks that composed the downtown district. Window shopping for a while, they came to the town park, smiled at old men who were sitting at a table playing checkers, saw two churches on opposite sides of the street. One was a large stone Episcopal with a gorgeous rose window. The other was a brick colonial-styled Methodist church. They walked back past the public library and stepped inside for a few minutes. Grandma made it a habit to visit libraries where ever she traveled and had a scrapbook collection of bookmarks since libraries almost always gave away bookmarks. Sure enough, she scored two bookmarks and a couple used books in grab bags that were a fundraiser by the Library friends. You got a brown paper bag stapled shut and inside were two books in whatever genre you chose, plus a Hershey's kiss and a bookmark. They were a dollar, so grandma got one for herself in the historical genre, and she got Annie one in the youth genre. They opened them on their way out.

"My goodness!" exclaimed grandma as she pulled out her two books. "The cover of this one needs to be censored." It had a naked to the waist and a bit below cowboy who was supposedly leading people across the country during the Oregon trail period.

"Dressed like that, I don't care how many muscles he's got, he'd never make it across the plains", she remarked. "Don't believe he's got the right stuff."

The other cover was of a young lady in a full ball gown, sweeping downstairs in a mansion during the early 1800's in England. "How are yours?"

"Well, I got one of the Black Stallion books by Walter Farley and that's good, I like his stuff and I don't have this one. This one I haven't read by Riordon so I've got two books I can read while we're here and maybe donate back? No reason they can't resell them after I've enjoyed them. I need to save my luggage weight for real souvenirs."

"Like the way you think, child," smiled grandma. "Well, we're almost home, let's lay out the refreshments for the girls. I can't wait to see Imelda and Frankie again. I went to school with them and they're just the best of friends."

"So how come you don't live up here?" asked her granddaughter.

"Friends are good, but family is better," smiled her grandma. "We can lay out the stuff and get started ourselves. With the six of us, quilting ought to go pretty quickly."

Chapter Three

Fed Ex handed the small package to the dispatcher.

"Hey, Becky, insured from the airport, overnight, directly for Erick," he announced.

"Thanks, Bill. Erick talked to them on the phone yesterday. I'll sign for it; he's in a meeting. Anything else?"

"Just a couple envelopes from the lab in Columbus. This one's heavy, careful. Sign here." As she signed, he asked, "Any word from Brad?

"Give him a break; it's the third day of his honeymoon and they haven't come up for air yet."

"Guess, not," he grinned. "I hope they're happy. They both been lonely for a long time." He took his sign-in tablet and left.

The receptionist ran the letters through the scanner, opened them and then set them in the sheriff's basket.

Jed came in from rounds. Just as he got to the desk, Becky answered the phone. She held up her hand to Jed, pausing him.

"Jed, sorry, you need to go back out. Call from 207 Main street. The furniture factory has been hit."

"On my way." He exited.

Erick came out of the office.

"Another hit it appears at the furniture factory." She announced to him as he picked up his mail.

"That's not on Main Street proper." Erick's face was heavy and he shook his head. "It's back is to Main street but it's behind the others. Wonder how the post office numbered that and why the perp chose that place."

"I guess because the factory front of it faces an alley and the back opens onto a small parking lot between the fire department and the hardware. Horses tie up there. Odd way to build."

"Building been there forever," commented the Sheriff. "Package from the airport show up?"

"Yeah, right here and from the lab. I think it's the results of that tablet they found in the church."

"Been long enough. They really have to hire in more geeks down there in Columbus."

"They're graduating them from police academy as fast as they can," replied Troy coming in. "It's not easy to find a good geek. What is that?"

"The quilt block found on the landing gear of the plane that nearly blew the Armstrong's to kingdom come. And where have you been? We got worried when you didn't get right back." Troy looked surprised.

"Sorry. I stopped for a McD's on the way back and went to my hotel room for bed. Been up since 5 am and it was seven-thirty when I left the airport. I hadn't eaten since 5:30 yesterday morning and I was pretty whipped. Long day and didn't realize I was on a schedule. Brad and his wife got off ok, I dropped them off and left, got a sandwich, headed back to my room because it was closer there than here. I checked out by email to the main office."

"Odd the office didn't manage to let us know," remarked Eric as he looked at the block. "Brad checked in once they got to their destination or we'd have gone out looking for you. This note says there was trouble on the plane, they had to board another, and this block is called Cain and Able. If it weren't a crime scene block, I'd say it's pretty." He took it to the back, copied it, surreptitiously send a copy to the Fabric Avalanche, and pinned the paper copy to the wall. The actual block went into an evidence bag and was put in the file.

"I don't get it. Neither the airport nor this block was anywhere on Main Street. Miriam said Brad was a target, but he was nowhere near here when attacked and a plane hijack doesn't fit this at all. Our perp is breaking his pattern."

Ally stood beside him. She studied awhile, then took the quilt square and moved it.

"Color wise, it goes over here; what's here in town?"

The sheriff went over to the town map. "The Hardware store. Casey and her brother own the Hardware store."

Voices came from the front room.

"I've got to see the Sheriff now," demanded a young man. Erick headed out front.

"It's OK, Becky. What's the matter, Matthew?"

"Sheriff, I got to the store this morning and this was painted on the back wall outside." He held up his phone. "I took a picture. And they superglued a toy airplane to the wall in the middle of the painting."

On the back wall of the hardware, the Cain and Able block blossomed about six feet across. In the center square was glued a foot-wide model of a Rutan V-tail puddle jumper.

"I'll send someone right over. Was the store broken into?"

"No. And I haven't been out back in a couple of days so don't know how long this has been here."

"I'm guessing the night of the wedding," replied Erick. "He must have known, never mind. Jed's out on a case."

"I'll go," began Troy.

"No, need you on the station. Carl? You in yet? Good! Head over and gather evidence at the Hardware store, get it back here. Good Lord, it's not even ten o'clock."

Chapter Four

Jed stood in the furniture store and frowned. He was surrounded by Amish men in solid-colored working shirts and pants, suspenders and straw hats, also frowning, arms folded over their chests, brows lowered, for all the world like a group of a frustrated wolf pack, not quite growling but definitely intimidating. Jed studied the wall assiduously.

"Wife might appreciate the art, but I am not understanding it," said one long-bearded man with grey hair. He was looking at the back wall of his shop where a six-foot-wide quilt block starred back at him.

"I don't know, Enoch, it's kind of pretty if you can get used to it. And it won't get dirty up there. The little one we found is apt to get pretty dusty tied to your table saw."

"Little one?" asked Jed.

"Ya, we left it all just as we found it. We all went away to lunch and came back and here it was. Paint's dry which is really strange. We can't have been gone what, an hour?"

"Long enough for them to gouge several of our pieces, tie the fabric there on the table saw and paint that wall?" The deputy got closer. "I don't believe that's paint, I think that's a big plastic decal, sort of like the ones they use for the annual barn tour...barn tour?" he thought a moment. "Let me get some pictures, and I think we can peel that off and take it with me. It might just explain some things." He went around, taking pictures, putting evidence in his bag.

"Any of you fellows smoke?"

"Na, but we had a client in here this morning ordered a table and chairs and we had to ask him to put out his cigarette. Could belong to him." Jed put the stub in an evidence bag. He went up to the large square and checked to see if it would peel. It easily came off: he got on a stool and rolled it up and at the top found two small tacks he put in an evidence bag and got back off the ladder.

"That's about it, guys. I'm sorry they ruined some of your work."

"Well, it was only a couple small tables he gouged and a lazy Susan. I think we can let the apprentices practice sanding them and we can put them on sale, lessened I need to keep them as evidence?"

"Don't repair them quite yet. Let me ask the Sheriff, but ought to be able to let you know. Everything else OK here and at your homes?"

"Everyone is sort of battened down," replied Enoch. "The wife is finally sleeping at night without nightmares."

Jed nodded. "That's good. I'm so glad Miriam wasn't harmed. Awful scare though. Has she gone back to work at the quilt shop?"

"She thought to start back this week, just part-time," Enoch replied. "She does so love being in there with the ladies a couple of days a week, and she likes to sew. It's not been dangerous until these last months. Oh, and I think I know that pattern."

"I do too," replied Elijah, the owner of the shop. "It's called Carpenter's Wheel. Miriam made us a couple of that pattern to carry here in the shop and keep us warm, just lap quilts." He went over to his office and came out with a bright purple, blue and cream lap quilt." Not the same color but see, here at the bottom she signed it. She gave it to me for the anniversary of the shop. We been here 25 years last year and the wives all made lap quilts and we had them hung all over the shop showroom: brightened it all up and we sold them at raffle to raise money for the school. Went really well, we raised over two thousand dollars and put the new roof on the school building. I got to keep this one though, see it says "In remembrance of twenty-five years of excellence in furniture making and service to our people. I'm right attached to it. I keep it in my office."

"It's really nice. Enoch, your wife is gifted. Course, I think all the ladies are gifts. Anyway, I'm going to take this all back to the station and if you see anything else odd, or someone you don't think is up to good, you let us know."

"I sure hope you catch this person," replied Enoch.

Jed nodded and headed out. Arriving at the station, he nodded to Becky and went to the back office.

"Here's the block for the furniture store," he started. "And look at what else we have." He unrolled the six-foot square.

The feds looked at it puzzled. "He's making decals now?"

"No," Jed said patiently. "Every other year as part of founders day, we get these decals made up and we put them on barns for the barn tour as part of the festivities."

Light began to dawn on the Sheriff's face. "So, if he had decals made up every time he's left one of these, we can get in touch with the folks who make these and maybe figure this all out by whoever has been ordering them? I mean a lot of folks didn't bother to try and take down the quilt blocks on the walls, they just left them up. I wonder how many are actually decals?"

"Absolutely. Who's in charge of the barn tour?"

"That would be Melissa Berring," the Sheriff sat down. "Dad blast it all! She's still in a coma at the hospital. She orders those somewhere each time we do the barn tour; we started out with five barns and now there are over a dozen. Some of the farmers opt to keep the decals and they pay the town back and leave them up, like over at David's family farm. The rest she stores and reuses. I wonder where she stores them?"

"I wonder if that's why she was injured," replied Ally. "She might be able to ID the perp."

"That is entirely possible," said the Sheriff. "Last report I got they were hoping she'd come out of it tomorrow: she's been giving them some sort of signs she might. We need to set protection on her. Becky!" he called out.

"Erick, you could use the intercom and not bellow like a bull."

"Bellowing's faster. Listen, get Franklin county online for me. I have some surveillance in their neck of the woods to be done. And after that, I need to talk to the Mayor. He may know where the barn tour stuff is kept."

Chapter Five

In the early morning, Brad hiked up the trail under tropical palms, laughing out loud as Casey surged ahead to get to the waterfall first. They'd come out just after breakfast and met almost no one on the trail, just as Chuck had suggested. He'd told them by afternoon, it would be crowded with tourists.

She breached out of the trees and stood, waiting for him, her eyes wide as she looked at the cascade falling into a deep azure pool, with white and gold sands sparkling in the sunlight.

"Oh, Brad, I wish we could take this home!" She exclaimed.

"'Fraid there's no way to keep it at home," he smiled. "A video of it will need to do. Look at those flowers!" he exclaimed as he shot pictures.

"And just smell them!" she said. "I thought the snorkeling was fun and the reef is beautiful, but this is just so gorgeous." She continued down the path, smelling flowers here and there, until she got to the water. "That sign over there says we're allowed to swim and to follow the path to go behind the waterfall. I've never been behind one."

"Then let's check that out. However, we do need to get back to the room before noon."

"Why?"

"I have something else planned for this afternoon."

"What could be better than this?"

"Oh, you'll see shortly."

Behind the falls, it was cooler, damper and looking through the sheen of the water was beautiful. "It's surprising how much force it has," remarked Brad. He leaned over and kissed her. She snuggled up into his arms and looked out through the wall of water. The watery cocoon felt safe and looking through the water she could see a double rainbow over the water pool.

"Thanks so much for thinking of coming here for our honeymoon." She said quietly. "I've never been any place like it. All the flowers and the water and just the sheer beauty of this place is simply captivating."

Brad nodded. "I've wanted to come ever since my buddy moved here. He's been after me for years and he gave me all these wonderful suggestions. He's been spot on so far on what we'd like." He nuzzled her neck. "And I for one will be glad to get back to our room this evening. But for now, let's continue this path, and then go home and we'll head out for the next surprise."

"Sounds fine." Hand in hand, they followed the path a couple more miles, seeing two more waterfalls, taking pictures, and short videos they sent home to Annie.

They arrived back at the parking lot and drove back to the house slowly, looking at the ocean and the white sands. Traffic was slowly picking up by the time they got home.

Brad suggested she get into something a little more formal than a bikini for their next stop.

"Formal like how? And I thought you liked bikini's?"

"Like shopping formal."

"We're going shopping?"

"Well, sort of; you'll need this." He held out a sewing box.

"A sewing box? Where exactly are we going?"

"How do you feel about sea turtles?"

"Sea turtles? And a sewing box. Brad, what are you planning?"

"Get dressed and come on out to the car. I think you're going to love this." Both of them changed from swimwear to casual shirts and shorts, walking shoes and beach hats. Casey grabbed her purse and they went out and got into the small green electric car he'd rented. She'd teased him about it at first, saying it looked like one of those pictures she'd seen of lily feet, the Chinese bound feet of the upper classes in China. She'd grown fond of the little car; it was totally quiet as it puttered along, and the idea that they were not polluting anything as they drove appealed to the ecologist in her. They drove along with the windows down, enjoying the scenery. Entering the small town of Kihei, he turned into a parking lot in a small mall, parking just in front of a quilt shop.

"A quilt store? Lovely!"

"Remember Candy said her mom owns a B&B and she does quilts? Well, she and Chuck have arranged a little surprise for you."

"Surprise?"

Brad led her into the store where a beaming Candy threw a lei around Casey's neck and hugged her.

"Aloha!" she and several other ladies cried. "Welcome to our quilt club meeting, Maui style. Now, Brad, shoo. We get her all to ourselves for the next few hours. Chuck's waiting to take you deep sea fishing." Two ladies all but dragged Brad outside where he got into Chuck's truck laughing and shaking his head.

"You're in the islands and the islands have traditions about newlyweds," exclaimed one lady. "And I'm Marla. Did you open your sewing box?"

"No, I hadn't."

"Well, go it now!" grinned an older lady. "This is our version of a wedding shower. Brad told Chuck a little of how you were squeegeed out of a proper wedding by hoodlums and we thought we'd try and make up some of it by introducing you to our wedding traditions. Now open the box."

Casey opened her pretty, woven sewing box. Inside were several envelopes, all numbered.

"We start with one, which is here," announced the owner of the shop. "Come along to the fabric. You need to pick three you really like, two you like but not as much and one or two others just for fun. What's your favorite color?"

"Your shop is lovely," exclaimed Casey. "My favorite color is sort of teal, well, mostly jewel tones and I love batiks and I will choose some fabric to take home but we won't have a lot of space."

"No buts. This is just the start and the fabric you choose is going to be put in use immediately."

"For what?" asked Casey.

"You'll see at the end of the day. Now you said you like batiks? Let's start there."

Urged on by the women, who seemed to keep coming out of nowhere until there were at least a dozen surrounding her, Casey walked around, choosing some beautiful island prints and batiks to match them. Each time she indicated a favorite, they took the bolt down and sat it over on the cutting table.

"Marvelous. Now based on what you just choose we'll know just what to do. Brad's provided us with some photos so we'll get started and you open envelop 2." declared Candy.

"It says Spa?"

"Grand, I thought so," Candy replied. "We'll see all you ladies in a little while. Casey, leave the basket, give me all the envelopes and let's get going."

Casey sat her green and gold basket down, took out the envelopes and handed them to Candy.

"Where to?"

"The spa of course. It's just a few stores down."

"Spa?" asked a dazed Casey.

Candy led her along.

"Yes, in our traditions, the new bride had a few days with her hubby and then the ladies did sort of a shower for her and pampered her a bunch and brought her back all dolled up for her husband for the second half of the honeymoon. We're doing all the dolling up and you won't know yourself by the end of the day. I'm our version of your matron of honor; normally it would be one of your adult female relatives, but I'll just have to do. I'm in charge of getting you to all the events, making sure things get done and watching the time so you aren't late for your luau. Here we are, Tiku's spa. And they're waiting for us."

Inside the spa, three smiling ladies welcomed Casey in and exclaimed over how the sun was drying her skin and she simply had to have a massage. Taking her back, Casey was given a really relaxing massage by a gently talkative person named Angel. She actually fell asleep for a few minutes as she was rubbed, soothed by soft music, and had warm rocks laid on the tight muscles she didn't know had been tight. A soft gong woke her and she sat up.

"Oh, that felt lovely," she exclaimed. "Please thank the ladies for me Candy, um, Candy?" Candy yawned. "Yep, we all need these at least every week. You have a good masseuse back home?"

"I didn't but I am definitely looking one up." One of the owners came back, suggesting they dress and come out for their facials, manicures and pedicures.

"All of that? Really? By ladies who don't even know me from Adam and Eve?"

"It's tradition!" laughed Candy. "I'm your guide to make sure it's all done properly. It's a community honor thing. Having fun so far?"

"Oh, for sure. Brad can't possibly be having as much fun on a boat fishing for who knows what. He is safe, isn't he?"

"Oh, he's getting his own version of this. He may or not make it to the boat."

'What? He thinks he's going fishing."

"Oh, Chuck's friends are doing the male drumming and feasting and then hiking him up a volcano thing with him. He's having fun but probably as confused as you are."

"Hiking up a volcano?"

"It's dead. He has to choose a special rock."

"A rock?"

"Uh, hum. He'll be shown how to take it or a shell and drill a hole in it and make you a necklace. It's part of being a good husband."

"You are kidding, right?" The ladies doing her nails burst out laughing. "I do so love people from the mainland when they come into this," the manicurist looked delighted. "It's all in good fun and when he comes to pick you up to head for the luau, he'll be bringing you gifts as is fit for a man of his stature in the village."

"Gifts?"

'Uh hum," beamed the woman. "Now do you like this particular shade? It glimmers and is called mermaid's tail, changes colors as you move your hands."

"Why not?" Casey replied. "I am beginning to feel a little like I'm in a fantasy."

"No worries. You have lovely feet," said the pedicurist. She completed her pedicure and spritzed perfume on Casey's feet. "There. Now you had tennis shoes on when you came in. May I suggest you wear these sandals? That way you can show off your pretty feet."

The sandals in question were of soft ivory leather, lacey and open toed, nicely padded for walking, fit perfectly and her feet did look pretty in them.

"I can't imagine what all these costs you ladies," Casey started with a worried look on her face.

"No to worry," smiled Candy. "And yes, the sandals are included. Open the next envelope."

Her next envelope took her to a hair salon, where she had her hair trimmed just a little, conditioned and given a temporary streaked color treatment in blues and greens and purples, then styled into waterfall braids, with some hair carefully styled at the top of each braid to look like a rose. Her hair was spritzed with glitter and she looked at herself in the mirror.

"I do not recognize me," she exclaimed. "I normally just tie my hair up in a ponytail or wear it in a French braid, but this is incredible. I can't wait until Brad sees it. Would you mind taking a picture front and back so I can send it to mom?" she asked Casey.

"Absolutely." Casey clicked a couple pictures, and sent them off to Mrs. Armstrong back home.

"Would you like me to show you the trick?" asked the chatty, friendly beautician.

"I would love that," replied Casey.

The woman walked into the back of her shop and came back with a long-haired wig on a stand. "One of the things we do is to train the bride to do her own hair so she can recreate it herself on her anniversary. Here's how a waterfall is done," she showed the details of her refined braid technique to Casey, had her do it several times on the manikin and satisfied, gave her a smile, a hug and another lei and sent her on her way.

"She was so nice!" exclaimed Casey as they left. "I am actually getting hungry. It must be at least three or so?"

"The luau is hours away yet and you have three envelopes and I've got to admit to being starved as well. What's next?" demanded Candy. "Here's envelope four."

"It says good for two complete lunches at the Homemade Café?"

"That's just around the corner and it's just in time! I'm starved and like I say, the luau is hours away. Let's eat! They have the best loco moco."

"Excuse me?"

"You'll see. And for sure shaved ice for dessert.,"

"Dessert?"

"You have three more envelopes, girl. We gotta have energy."

Loco moco turned out to be a dish made with hamburger, eggs and gravy over jasmine rice. Casey opted to have a veggie pot pie and lemonade. After lunch she opened her next envelope.

"All it says is Shop! In big letters and has gift cards to three places."

"Tradition says you need to give your parents and close relatives little gifts to remember that you still love them, so the gifts cards are for getting small things to take home to your mom and Casey. These three little shops are close by."

"How much can we actually carry home? I mean, you know Chuck's airplane…"

"We have the plane so there is room for just about everything except a baby elephant. Let's go. What does Annie like?"

For the next hour and a half, Casey and Candy chatted their way through three gifts shops, picking up a yarn bowl with matching mother of pearl yarn stitch counters and 700 yards of incredibly soft bamboo and silk yarn in a scrumptious variegated sea green, blue, and deep purple color for her mother. For Annie, she bought a funny t-shirt, abalone necklace with matching earrings that were shaped like dolphins and a small bell from the islands. "Annie collects bells whenever we go on travels. She has ten of them now but she hasn't got one from here."

"Let's add a lei made of sea shells for her and your mom."

"They'd like that." Purchases made, they went outside and pulled out another envelope.

"It says, Proceed to Ahikiku shop. What on earth?" asked Casey.

"Here's where you get to look authentic."

"I don't look authentic now?"

"No, the traditional bride, the wahini, wore a sort of muu-muuish sort of dress, usually brightly patterned in the old days but pretty much white now. We need to get you dressed for your wedding luau and the sandals will do just fine." She led Casey into a store where they were once again met by the owner who offered her good wishes on her special day and helped her change into a very flowing, white embroidered with ivory and rose flowers and green vines dress that seemed to swirl as she walked. Candy added a silver bracelet. "Brad will be wearing the same print fabric by the time the guys are done with him," she smiled. "It's tradition to match. Oh, and he'll be wearing the same bracelet too, only bigger. Also tradition. Now, I'll carry your other clothing in this bag. We have one more stop before we get back to the quilt store."

"What could we possibly need next? I have been pampered like a queen."

"You are a queen today," smiled Candy. "Queen of Brad's home and heart and best friend who saved my husband's life twice."

"What? I didn't know."

"Once in the military, once while a cop. Brad's a good man, a loyal person and one of the few folks I think My Chuck would die for, besides me and the little one coming. Here we are."

"A floral shop?"

"Open the envelop."

"It says, Pick up flowers?"

"Yes, the bride wears flowers in her hair, right above the waterfall braids, and a wrist corsage. Hi, Levi!" she called out as they entered the floral shop.

"Ah, the bride!" he exclaimed. "I have them right here." He went over to a flower fridge. "Now, please just sit down on this chair in front of this mirror.." The owner was a short, somewhat rotund, smiling man, appearing to be a traditional islander. "You are a lovely wahini," he exclaimed. He gently placed a floral haku-lei on her head, and settled it to stay with two or three hairpins. It was made mostly of very fragrant plumeria blossoms, and he put a floral corsage of the same flowers on her wrist.

"Let me look, silver bangle, floral corsage, lei on head and around neck, yes, just about done." Her phone rang. Candy checked it and smiled. "Just in time, let's head back to the quilt store.

"One moment please, if I may," said the florist. He held out a small bag to her. "In this box are six pots of plants you can keep in the house and grow: you can put them outside in the summer in full sun but in winter must bring them in. I have included the growing information. This is plumeria, ginger lily, hibiscus, bird of paradise, an orchid and a proteria. I heard you like to garden and I thought perhaps you would enjoy these as a gift from our hearts to yours."

"Oh, thank you!" exclaimed Casey. "They're lovely. Are you sure They will make the flight safely?"

"When you get ready to go, put this cover on the box to keep them safe. Until you go, keep them on your patio, water them every other day."

"Levi, thank you as well. We weren't expecting that!"

He bowed slightly.

"I'll just sit these in the back seat of the car before we go into the shop. Aren't they lovely?" Candy beamed. "Now, here we are, wait for me a second." She slid the flowers into the back seat. The ladies from the shop spilled out and exclaimed at her, laughing and smiling and patting her back.

"While you have the door open, this box of fabric goes with her too, to make quilts with during the cold Ohio winters and to remember our warm beaches," proclaimed the shop owner. "And your sewing box is full of notions. And most of all, we made this for you." Three of the ladies suddenly spread out and held up a full-size quilt, done in the fabrics she had chosen, in a traditional style. The background was a batik, and the appliqued flowers and turtles, palms and pineapples were breathtakingly and expertly embroidered into place.

"You did this entire quilt this afternoon"? gasped Casey. "And quilted and backed and bound it as well?"

"Many hands make light work," smiled the shop owner. "It's tradition to gift the new bride with a blanket for her bed. We just decided it needed to be a quilt since you're a quilter. Do you like it?"

"I am in love with it."

"We made it a queen size since that's pretty standard here. Will that fit your bed back home?"

"We have a queen size bed back home so it's perfect. I don't know how to thank you."

"Well, now you have to thank us by sewing with us for an hour. We have the pieces cut out and we are going to help you make a gift for Brad."

"Let me guess, tradition?"

"Absolutely," they all laughed. "We thought maybe a couple potholders? That's to remind him to help in the kitchen. We've got the patterns all cut out and you just need to help us all sew them together."

"All of us? How many potholders are we talking here?" Casey said uneasily.

The ladies all started giggling and swept her into the store.

Chapter Six

Mike walked into the sheriff's office along with his son Alan.

"It had to happen eventually," he began. "I need to see the Sheriff," he announced to Becky.

"About?" she asked.

Wordlessly, Mike held up a quilt block. Becky rang Erick.

The sheriff, flanked by Jed and Ally, came out of the back office.

"Well, guess that answers that question," remarked Erick as he slid the next square into an evidence bag. "We wondered if the crook would consider you part of the other three shops but guess not. Jed, would you go over and see what happened over at the museum?"

"Suzanne saw me pull it out, looked at it and said it was a Friday the Thirteenth square. It's not in the original quilt."

Mike ran the Not Your Normal Antique store, which was attached to his wife Allyssa's yarn store, the Fiber Mavens. Thom's Hobbies was on the other side of the four-store building and had been hit first by the unknown thugs who had been trying to terrorize the little town. Mike's son, Alan, was attacked but fought off the attacker. Miriam, who worked at the Fabric Avalanche, the next store over, had been kidnapped but returned safely. The police had hoped an attack and a kidnapping had been all that was going to happen to these popular shops, but the stores were obviously still on the villain's mind.

"Anything stolen or broken? Anyone hurt?" asked Ally.

"I saw the square tucked up in the mailbox slot and didn't open the door," Mike admitted. "I wasn't sure they weren't still in there. I grabbed it and came straight here. Oh, but I asked Suzanne who was going to open up her shop from the front as well. She said that block is called Friday the Thirteenth. They're all waiting and Thom's pretty charged up."

"Jed, get evidence. Rest of you get back to tracking. Mike, sorry this happened and we'll be on it." Jed picked up his hat and headed out with Mike for the three-block hike down to the stores.

"Fits with your store, doesn't it?" replied Jed as he walked down the street with Mike and Alan. "I mean, Friday the Thirteenth and that mummy you have and that articulated hand thingy and such."

"Also lots of just plain neat stuff," retorted Alan as he walked next to his dad. "I thought we were relatively safe, I mean, he attacked me and I figured that covered Dad's store."

"Guess not," replied his dad. "Here we are. The block was sitting in the mail slot there. I haven't opened up yet."

Two or three people came over. "Hey, Mike, you OK?" asked Finian.

"They get you too?" asked another passerby.

"Nothing to see here," replied Jed firmly. "We don't know anything's wrong but we're heading inside."

"If nothing's wrong, how come none of these four stores are open?" demanded a lady. "Stores close when they're in trouble."

"I don't see trouble, could be they're setting up a Founder's Day sale. You all can check back later. Now, please just go about your business." said Jed firmly. He shooed them away, then nodded for Mike to unlock his door.

"Don't you normally open at the rear?" Jed asked.

"No, I like to get in from here and see the store just as the customers would if they walked in first thing," he said. "I stand here, take a breath, look around and go make adjustments. Then I go in back and open the safe and get the cash drawers for us all and we all get started."

Thom, Allyssa, and Suzanne, Miriam and Lydia were waiting in the archway between their stores and his. "Everything ok? We opened our places up except for the front doors but waited over here," asked Suzanne.

"We haven't checked yet to see what's going on. Maybe, maybe not. I found a block so I got the deputy here to open with me." Mike stood in the front, looked all around and took a sharp breath.

"Someone's broken that display: the glass is busted."
He walked over to the cash register display counter, which
was glass. Someone had indeed broken it. "My cat mummy is
gone. And look back there." He pointed. Hung up across the
back door was a six-foot reproduction of the Friday the
Thirteenth square. Jed walked around taking pictures, sending
them over to the Sheriff's office. He checked and saw the
decal was pinned up, not installed, so he gently rolled it up.
Behind it, someone had graffitied the walls and doors of the
back area with slogans.

"Semper Fi; You can fly but can't hide; bread or roses,
Nothing to Fear but Me, You will pay," were some of them, in
bright, lime green paint across walls, the floor, the boxes
stocked up. Jed found the paint spray can in a trash can and
put it in a bag.

"I can call friends and we can help clean it," said Lydia.

"It only appears that this store was hit, not the other
three, I assume you've checked that?"

They all nodded. "OK, but your storage rooms back
here are all one large one area, you sort of share the space so
let's check out your inventories and such," said Jed.

"My buddies Bob and Charlie were here on sleepover
last night and we didn't hear anything," said Alan. "Mrs.
Harmony is not out and about yet so I didn't ask her. She lives
right next-door upstairs. Today was teacher in- service so we
guys didn't have school but they both have jobs and left to go
to work early. We should have heard the glass breaking."

"Not necessarily," answered the deputy. "Glass can be
broken quietly if you're careful. How valuable was the cat
mummy? Is there anything else gone?"

Mike shook his head. "I picked that up when I was in the service and stationed in the Middle East way back in the '90s. I have an insurance value placed on it of $25,000. A guy came in once and offered me $5000 for it and I checked with a couple of museums and dealers and decided to insure it for that much. I only paid fifty bucks for it from a booth over in Cairo. He had several and I just thought it was cool." The deputy wrote it all down.

"Anyone find anything else?" Mike was walking around checking things here and there, wandered in back where Thom and Suzanne had checked around.

"It appears he came in by the back door," replied Mike. "Door lock has been jimmied and broken. I'll get a locksmith over here today to fix it."

"Mike, after they're done, I have a spare counter cabinet in back. When they're done with forensics, let's you, me and Alan switch out the one with the broken glass and be thinking about what you want to replace the cat display with there."

Mike nodded.

"Let me get the guys over to dust first, then locksmith and whoever else can come," Jed stepped outdoors and looked at the four back doors. I'm setting up crime tape from this door to that one."

"Guys, check and see if the doors are all locked."

"Already checked. They are," answered Thom.

"Did you guys all come in the front?"

"We did. We've been doing that thinking it might be safer than coming in the back, for the ladies at least, since it's right out front on the street," replied Suzanne.

"OK, you guys come out here. You need to identify something for me."

There between the doors on the walls were two more blocks, the matching decals to the first blocks that had been left in the first attacks; Arkansas Traveler on Thom's wall, Sailboat on Suzanne's. Allyssa's wall space was blank. Thom's mouth dropped open; Suzanne turned pale.

"Alyssa, I think we need to add more security to your place," Thom replied. "It's evident the perp now considers them separate stores and yours hasn't been hit."

"You don't think Mrs. Harmony's dog Pierre being killed wasn't an attack? She lives right upstairs."

Jed shook his head. "Appears to me they've decided not. These decals are reminders he can be here anytime and we won't know. He's rubbing our faces in it. I have no idea why. I do know we need to get the forensics guys over here."

"They've not been much help so far."

"Yeah, but Homeland sent us a team to stay here. They're pretty thorough and I've called them already. That ought to be them coming in through the door now. We'll try to get your stores open quickly as we can. No need upsetting the town anymore."

"I'm going to call the ladies and cancel the noon classes," said Suzanne. "Allyssa?"

"Me, too, I guess. I hate this." The forensics folks went over all four stores, dusting, looking for blood. They especially studied the broken case. As soon as they gave the all-clear, Mike, Thom, and Alan moved the broken cabinet to the back for repair, moved the newer one out front and got a display out of ancient pottery lamps to put inside, and another small display of Indian arrowheads that had been found locally, all labeled with the farms they'd been found on and the estimated age. By one, the stores were open for tourists again. The back room was being scrubbed and rearranged by Amish ladies, and the locksmith put stronger locks on all four back doors. With everyone so curious about the very public break-in, the locals swarmed the store, commiserating, fussing and sympathizing. Tourists seeing the commotion came as well. Financially, it was a really good day for everyone.

When the last tourist left, Thom tallied his drawers and got his deposit ready.

"We ought to stage a few more break-ins," he declared. "I've got to stay late and put out more stock, wife."

"I've run out of some fabrics, the kits are depleted, and I've got to get online to my suppliers to send another order of notions and kits in. I wasn't expecting to do this good until Founder's Day when all the busses come," she replied. "It's been busy but my land, what a day! Lydia, you were a godsend! Thank you so much for getting your friends to come in and clean! Is the driver here already?"

"Yes, Ma'am, he's out back so we're all leaving. I'll see you Wednesday," she smiled.

"Oh, wait, didn't you say you needed some lengths of blue and brown fabric? I got them cut off, and where did I lay them? Oh, here they are." She handed her some fabric. "No need to pay; consider them a bonus. Hug those kinner for me."

"Denki, thank you!" exclaimed Lydia. "Are you for certain?"

"Absolutely. If we hadn't canceled out our classes we'd never have gotten through the day."

"Miriam, I have some fabric for you as well, you like burgundy and needed black, yes?"

"We do."

"Excellent," smiled Suzanne. "Allyssa? How are you doing?"

"I have not had a day like that since before Christmas and we had extra help. However, a few days like that and we'll balance out the entire year! I am, however, looking forward to a hot bath and getting off my feet. I'm coming in early tomorrow to get things set up. Thom and Mike, can you check all the doors and be sure they're tight?"

"Already done. Let's get going. Son, you want to join us for supper at Ricci's?"

"No question. I could eat an entire pan of lasagna by myself," he declared. "My apartment's locked, so let's go."

"I want to just run up and check on Mrs. Harmony," answered his dad. "I'll be sure everything's OK up there. I'll catch up."

Thom caught Mrs. Harmony getting ready to head for "that noodle place" as she called Ricci's so she opted to walk with Thom. He noticed the puppy in her handbag. "A puppy! What cute little guy! When did you get him?"

"My friend Mazie's bitch had a litter of poodles and she let me pick the one I wanted to replace poor Pierre. His name is Bronson."

"Bronson?"

"Yep, I'm saving up for a trip to see John Anderson next fall. I do love country music." Thom laughed and helped the feisty old lady downstairs, being sure she locked up first.

Chapter Seven

Marie Clamons sat in her chair and mulled over the events of the last few days.

I simply can't see why anyone would do this. I never wanted anyone to get hurt because I quilt. I'm glad Toby took down the website or gave it over to the FBI or whomever those folks were. I don't know as to how I can keep making blocks for it. They want me to see if they can trace any new orders but oh, dear! How can I possibly do that? The ladies over at the shop are quilting the ones for Liam and Toby and they'll be done in time to give the boys but how can I plan more blocks right now? I am just so aggravated about this entire thing. Oh! Someone's at the door. Toby's not here, where is that cane? Here it is.

"Coming!" She called out. "I'm coming, I don't move so fast anymore." *I suspect it's the hospice folks come to talk. Such nice folks.*

Marie opened the door to find Liam and a tall young man next to him.

"Liam, what a nice surprise. And who is this?" she looked at him closely. "Wait, is it Matthew? After all these years?"

"Hi, ma," said the tall young man. "Liam called me and said you were ill and explained stuff and I just wanted to see you, that's all. Can I come in?"

"Of course, of course, come in, Liam, how on earth..." Liam leaned over and kissed her on the cheek.

"Just a quick visit, mom. I wanted some amends to be made and I wanted to see you. I'll be going away for a while and wanted to talk about it."

"Away? But you have the shop and the baby coming and everything. What is going on?"

"Mom, we need to talk," began Matthew. "First, I need to explain what's been happening with me over the last few months. You see, when dad took us, he did some pretty bad things and really ruined our reputation as a family. There wasn't just what he did to you and us, but he cheated and defrauded a bunch of folks. If he weren't dead, he'd be in jail; the lawyers can only do so much. When I got married, I took my wife's maiden name, instead of her taking mine. I'm Matthew Solomon now. Matthew Clamons doesn't exist anymore. Jack destroyed him and what he didn't destroy, the war did a number on. It took me a long time to sort out his lies."

Marie took this in and shook her head as she sat down.

"So, all those letters coming back no such person, you got married? I didn't know you could do that, change your name instead of her."

"I'm married to a sweet woman named Havilah Solomon. She's an accountant and a good one. I work in Security. I have my own business and it goes well. Kevin, you know him as Toby's computer geek friend, he works with me. He's Havilah's brother. Havilah and I have two kids. I brought you a family picture." He handed her a framed picture showing himself, a dark-haired lady holding a baby and a toddler. "That's Esther in her arms and Eli. He's two and a half and handful. I don't know how we got him to hold still for the portrait. Great photographer, I guess."

"And you weren't mad at me all those years? Our last meeting wasn't really very quiet." Marie said quietly.

"I was an idiot, I was twenty-three and just out of the marines, I had PTSD from seeing Arthur blown up and I was just so angry at the world; I blamed everyone. I'd had six plastic surgeries to fix my face and arm and leg and I had to get my head screwed back on by a shrink. I met Havilah and got married and life settled down. I always felt bad that I hadn't come and apologized to you but I couldn't face this awful town and I was pretty ashamed. I just kept putting it off thinking I'd do it next time I was in town on a job and just didn't. I feel bad about waiting so long and when Liam called and said he needed help with a job and that you had cancer, something just sort of snapped into place inside and I decided to come to see you. Liam and I have a security job to do and it ought to clear dad's name in this town and maybe make it quieter for you."

"Clear dad's name? He left years ago. I doubt people even know of him."

"No, he left a lot of unfinished things, bills you had to pay, people who still remember, folks who made life hard for you while you and Toby struggled. Liam and I are going to clear the last record and then we have to go away for a little while. We've set up to be sure you're going to be OK, and Toby as well."

"Where are you going? I just got to see you and I want to meet your wife and my grandchildren."

"We won't be far and it won't be long until you meet up with us again. Liam's building a wing on his house and it's going to be done by Founder's Day. Are you going to the festivities?" Matthew asked, changing the subject.

"If I'm strong enough. Toby said he was going to ask Liam if he could get me a folding wheelchair so I could go."

"He did ask. It's out in the car. Did you know the Pastor's wife had a pumpkin bug like yours?"

"They're good little cars," smiled his mother. "That little car has stood the test of time. Got Toby to college and us to errands for years now. Pastor drives a Prius, one of those electric cars. I don't know about them. They don't sound normal."

"Well, you'll be glad to know Liam now has his own car." grinned Matthew. "His wife went and bought it."

"It's Marti's," Liam protested. "She needed it for the baby. Bugs don't have a lot of room for car seats." Matthew chuckled. Then he spoke to his mom seriously.

"Mom, before we head out, I wanted to go over some stuff with you. I know you had to sell a quilt to get money to take care of Toby and you've made him a new one. I saw the ladies quilting it for you and it's really pretty. I've been looking into getting the one you sold back from the museum but it appears they aren't interested in that. I know it's a lot to ask, but if you had blocks like the ones in that quilt, I could have my wife sew them up for me and we'd have matching quilts. I'd like that. It would be something to pass on to my son."

"Oh, I am so glad you asked!" exclaimed Marie. "Over there right next to that end table in the big plastic box, yes, that's the one, Liam. I have another quilt top all done. It's like the others. If you could drop it off at the quilt store, they could assemble it for us and all three of my boys will have quilts. I made one for all of you, even though Arthur is gone. His are the blocks I sold and they all got used in crimes and I don't know what to do about that. I can't figure out a way to make that right for the town. I feel like I had a part in a crime spree."

"That's nothing to be concerned about. There are some real sicko's out there and Toby said they'd shut down the website, so they'll just buy someone else's blocks to cause trouble with, and you're not to worry about it."

"Troy said that too. He's grown into such a nice man."

"For a half-brother," said Liam. "He was dad's second wife's boy and he was raised with us. That summer when she was sick and the aunt couldn't take care of us and we all came to stay here a few weeks, he said those were the best days of his life. He hated living with dad. We never got close since we were sent to live with our aunt. He was always asking questions about what life had been before we interloped on his mom's house and it all went to hell. Dad moved to her place and gambled away a lot, and the court sent us away to our aunt and Troy stayed with his mom, and when she kicked dad out, let's just say it was an awful mess. We met up again in the military and afterward, Troy went off to become an FBI agent. He's pretty much a straight shooter." Liam seemed to lose thought and ramble during this short speech to mom, he repeated himself and embellished a bit but took a deep breath as mom interrupted.

"I'm glad. Despite all the pain and the being poor, all my boys have turned out fine. I'm glad I lived in a small town where there were neighbors who helped out."

"What neighbors helped?" asked Liam. "I remember the sale and I remember they snatched up our things for pennies of what they were worth and losing everything and then losing dad as well when we were sent away. I remember how embarrassed I was that a schoolteacher got our house, and that bank president, standing there on the steps as it all was sold, tallying up the money on a clipboard, shaking his head. That horrid sheriff, holding up stuff, sending it out to the bidders as they came up. It was awful, that day. And for the next few weeks, being teased at school about my idiot brother who wasn't perfect enough to come live in civilization. Our stepmom had a big house and good money. She lost a bunch of it to dad's gambling losses." Liam spoke quietly. "Toby had a lot of resentment for a long time, but he said when he got back, he saw how many of the folks were good to you. I'm glad he got to stay with you."

"He's been my rock all these years," said Marie. "But son, the town hasn't been bad. The Amish especially are so kind to me. They come by and bring me baked goods and last fall they gave me canned food and they are so friendly. And Mildred and Sophia have never quit being my friends. We get together to gossip at Sophia's house. Mildred lives in a little upstairs apartment with her yappy little dog and I can't climb so we just meet at Mildred's. But they said next week they'd come to my house for tea and sewing."

"Sophia is the old lady in the pink house, right?" asked Liam.

"Yes, it is. She's such a dear person."

Liam looked at Matthew who nodded.

"Well, we have to get along, now. We'll be seeing you soon, and mom, I'm glad you forgave me."

"I'm so glad you came. Liam, you tell that lady of yours thank you so much, oh, your casserole dish. She made me a casserole and we ate it all and the dish is in the kitchen."

"Don't get up, I'll get it." He leaned over and kissed her on top of her head. "Toby home soon?"

"Yes, in a couple of hours. The lady from Hospice is due any time now."

"Then we'll just get moving," replied Matthew. "We'll see you soon, mom."

After her boys left, Marie thought to herself. *They didn't tell me about the trip they were going on. I suppose it's business of some sort. They can't be gone long, Marti's due in early fall. Lord, keep my boys safe and thank you for finally bringing my family back together.*

Chapter Eight

Brad looked at Chuck, "Not fishing? Thought the whole reason I took Casey to the quilt store was so we could go fishing?"

Chuck grinned. "That's the cover story. You, my friend, are getting the bachelor party you never had."

"I'm not a bachelor. And I don't do alcohol or strippers. And I can't imagine why I'd need a bachelor party." Brad protested.

"Well, we do it differently in the islands. Look at it as sort of a coming of age, be a man, here's how you take good care of your wife thing."

"Excuse me?"

"In the islands, there's a tradition of a seven-day marriage feast. The first day, you're married, you go off alone for a few days but the sixth day, you all get together with family and friends, she goes with her friends who spend the day dolling her up and pampering her, and you go with your guy friends to be reminded of your manly duties to care for your new family and they end the day with a knock 'em dead luau. The luau is at seven tonight. So, we have eight hours to get you all properly gotten ready for the ceremony."

"What ceremony? We're married. I don't need a ceremony."

"Not in the islands, I mean by tradition, you have to be properly prepared for married life. You need to give her a present and dress properly and run through trials to show you're strong enough..."

"Trials?" asked Brad.

"Yeah, you know, snorkel with sharks, run up a volcano and jump in, that sort of thing." There was a long pause. Brad spoke first, slowly and with emphasis.

"Jump into a volcano? You are kidding, right?"

"Nope. We're not."

"We?" asked Brad.

"Here's the guys, waiting to join us." He pulled into a parking spot on the beach.

The "guys" cheered as Brad and Chuck got out of the car. Brad was practically carried to the beach, hauled out and tossed into the ocean.

"First, you gotta learn to surf," declared Chuck. "It sort of takes the place of swimming with sharks cause, who knows, there could be sharks out there but why take too many chances? By the way, this is Hugh, Olas, Barry, Dale, Dan, and Gabe. They're all good guys, work with me, drink with me and in general, love the islands. Now, this is a surfboard."

"I have to do this?" Brad asked. "I'm not exactly in a swimsuit."

"In the old days, all you'd wear was a sort of thong thing.,"

"I don't do thongs."

"OK, just leave your tennis shoes here, apt to be slippery on the board, fasten this around your ankle so we can find you when you fall off and paddle out to catch a wave."

"Are there actually sharks and we really have to do this?"

All the guys agreed and yelled almost as one, "It's tradition!"

Brad sighed, hopped up on the board and paddled out, surprising them all. He looked for his wave carefully, not dangling his feet in the water, then turned his board, waited as it caught, stood up and rode it in, gracefully boogieing it home and back to them.

"That was great!" declared Hugh. "Didn't know you could surf. Usually, it takes mainland guys longer to learn to ride it in."

"Sometimes we have to actually let them come in kneeling on the board," said Olas.

"I was a seal," said Brad. "I can do a lot more than surf and I'm not convinced I ought to start my marriage by lying to Casey." he paused. "But you say she's having fun getting dolled up for the party so let's get this done. Now what?"

"Let hit the volcano." Barry enthused. "That's always a blast."

Hustling Brad back to the parking lot, they all piled into the truck seat and the bed, tore out of the parking lot, waving white banners. Residents beeped back as they passed, yelled and laughed and began following them.

"What on earth?" asked Brad.

"Traditional islanders recognize what's going on and will join us to celebrate."

"Celebrate?"

"Everybody loves a groom here, most as much as his wahini, who is right now getting all dolled up for tonight-you know hair, nails, all that stuff women do. We have to get you ready for your luau."

"Luau?"

"Yep, wedding luau where you publicly declare your eternal love to Casey and eat too much, dance too much and are escorted home, serenaded and showered with flowers and gifts."

"You're joking right?" asked Brad as he looked out the back window and saw cars trailing him, honking, the drivers waving and yelling, wavering between the lanes, doing u-turns to join the party.

"Where are the cops? Those folks are driving like maniacs. How did we get so conspicuous?" he gulped as two police cars joined the parade, turned on their blinkers and followed along.

"Oh, traditional cops join right in. But only the folks who sort of know us are going to follow us around more than one stop, they won't last all day. Except to give you gifts at every stop."

"We have to fly home. How are we going to carry gifts?"

"Don't worry about it. If we ship them, I'll just end up doing the transport anyway. There's the volcano."

"You are really expecting me to jump into a volcano?" asked Brad. "I don't have any fire equipment."

"No worries, come on." They parked, Brad, surrounded by Chuck's six friends who hurried him up the side of a small mountain, were followed by a hoard of other men, chanting something in old Hawaiian.

As they reached the rim, Brad saw the volcano was actually an extinct crater. At the top was a restaurant and after taking a few pictures of Brad teetering on the edge, they hauled him inside where the bartender was waiting for him.

"Here you have it," he announced to no one in particular. "This drink is called lava flow. Groom gets first drink." Brad eyed it suspiciously. Chuck gave him a nod of encouragement. Brad lifted it, sniffed it and took a sip and then a swallow. "You know, this isn't too bad," he said. "One's my limit though. I'm not a big drinker."

"That's what all the friends are for!" declared Chuck. "Friends, everyone gets a drink on the groom!"

"Wait," gulped Brad as the men mobbed the bar, grabbing the drinks set up. "I have to pay for all these drinks? There must be a hundred men here."

"Where do you think the burn comes in?" asked Chuck. "No, seriously, me and the guys have already set the bill. That's why all those extra guys joined, for the free drinks. They're supposed to give you a blessing as soon as they've had theirs, so get ready. Better drink up so it doesn't get spilled. I told Bob the barkeep to halve the rum in it. Yours is mostly fruit juice."

"Thanks for the warning." He knocked back his last sip and sat his glass down on the bar as the first man came up and hugged him. "Noho me ka Hau'oli," he said as he pounded Brad's back. "Be happy, my son."

The next man shook his hand and then bear-hugged him, "Have a great life, man. Thanks for the drink."

"Ua ola loko i ke aloha" an older man, appearing Hawaiian, murmured and left.

Brad looked at Chuck. "Something about love being cleansing like dew," he muttered.

The line went on, everyone saying some blessings until all had left. The bartender came over and handed Brad an envelope. "This is from them all. Use it wisely to bring happiness to your family," he smiled. Inside the envelope seemed to be a lot of money.

"I don't understand." Brad looked thoroughly confused. "Don't I have to pay him? Why is he paying me?"

"Yes, you sat them up for drinks," said Chuck. "But they'd be less than good men if they didn't give you the money to pay the barkeep and have some leftover. What you see is a wedding gift from a bunch of total strangers who like weddings, right, Bob?"

"Yep, drinks are all paid for, you got a couple hundred left to use on your honeymoon."

Brad broke into a grin. "Maybe we ought to go rouse up another parade."

"Nope got to hurry on to the next thing. You need a facial."

"I need what?"

"Trust me on this."

They all hauled back to the road and drove into town to a barbershop. Brad got his hair trimmed, his nails trimmed and his hands softened with warm damp towels, a pumice rock rubbing out any calluses and sweet-smelling lotion massaged in. Then his face was wrapped in a warm towel for a few minutes. When he took off the towel, the man shaved Brad closer than he'd ever been, just short of taking off the first layer of skin, and slapped him with shaving lotion which smelled nice but tingled pretty badly. He was gifted another envelope that had a large shiny star on the front and the name of the shop.

He looked at Chuck. "Bad form for you to look in them from here on," remarked Chuck. "Just give them to me, I tuck them in this big envelope and they're put with your other gifts tonight at the luau. Let's see, next on the list is buying a gift for your relatives. You need to show them honor and remember them on your happy day. Who's your closest?"

"Guess my mom, my sister, and my aunt. Dad died years ago and I don't have any brothers, well, Casey has and technically, he's going to be a brother."

"You got their addresses so you can mail them out or do you want to give them to them yourself?"

"I have their addresses in my phone."

"Excellent. Ought not to take too long. Let's get to a souvenir shop and pick them and ship them out so that's done, and then we need to choose a nice gift for the wife, a couple of symbolic things for your house, and get you properly cleaned up for tonight."

"I thought the hair, nails, and jeez, what was that they did to my hands?"

"Defoliation to remind you your hands must always be soft because your wife is soft and doesn't deserve hard."

"If you say so. I could use a shower to get rid of the saltwater."

"Yep. That's in the plan." Chuck led the main group of guys out, they all walked to a local gift shop where a lei was thrown over Brad's neck so everyone would know he was the groom. Brad chose a bracelet and earrings for his sister, silver ones made to look like plumeria flowers. He got his mother a necklace made of gilded seashells with matching earrings. He got his aunt a sarong type fabric with a large orchid broach made of silver and gold inlaid with tiny semi-precious stones. He chose a wild Hawaiian shirt for his almost brother in law and a shark tooth necklace. All of his purchases were boxed up in front of him, he addressed labels and they were prepared to be posted that day with the mail.

"Got you here in time to hit the mail truck, so they'll go out tomorrow for the mainline and ought to have them by Friday," declared Chuck. "What are you looking at?"

"Chimes. Casey was saying she'd like chimes for the back porch at the farm. They have really long ones here." He walked over to the display. Touching them gently he discovered one very large bronze looking one had a bonging bass tone, like a gong. Another set that had six tubes sounding more mellow, still another, etched with dolphins and turtles was higher pitched. A fourth set was made of sea glass and tinkled as it sparkled.

"I think I'd like to get Casey chimes. Things to remember the sea and the islands with." The men around him nodded solemnly.

"That is a good thought," said Olas. "It would also give you something to give her for the house."

"I thought maybe some plants for the house. Here we normally plant a flower and a tree to grow with us, and then another when each child is born," said Gabe.

"Normally you gift the wife some jewelry or some cloth to make herself a dress, or something like that," agreed Chuck. "But chimes are good. Let's get all four."

"All four?"

"Sure, soprano, alto, tenor, bass. She'll have a quartet. And we'll go to a greenhouse for plants. And maybe other pretty things and," he checked his watch. "Guys, t minus three hours. We still have a lot to do."

"Yeah, and food would be good."

"Right, Lunch. Let's get something and I'll just take a minute and have the shopkeeper wrap these up for us. Dale, you run them back to the truck?"

"Sure. Going to Joes'?"

"Yeah, he's got great burgers and he's fast."

Adding the shopkeeper's envelope to the yellow envelope, Chuck and the guys made their way to Joe's burger Joint, got some sandwiches to go and headed back out to the truck. They drove to another shopping area and went into a greenhouse. After a discussion with the florist, Brad chose two mimosae, a jacaranda, a hibiscus, and a hardy banana tree. He added some Hawaiian tiki sculptures, a couple of pretty vases and a necklace made of sea glass. They loaded it all up and headed for the next place.

Chuck took him into another shop where he got Casey a special necklace to remember the night by: not that Brad would think she'd forget, not if she was doing all this stuff like he was. He chose a rose gold stingray on a sterling silver chain. For good measure, at Chuck's urging, he got her a bracelet and earring set to add to the gift pile.

The next stop was a men's store, but not one he'd seen the like of before. He was shooed into the back where he took a shower, being careful not to hurt his hairstyle, dried off and was handed clean underwear and a pair of chino shorts. The tailor handed him a white shirt with embroidered pink and rose flowers and vines, changed his tennis shoes for leather sandals, added a headpiece of flowers.

"I look nuts," said Brad looking in the mirror.

"You look like a groom, a kaho lio," answered Dan. "At the ceremony, your hands will be tied together at one point. And we will feast and see gifts and dance. You'll never forget it." Brad privately thought dressed like this was something he'd never forget and wondered what his dog would think.

Rutherford wouldn't recognize him by smell, looks and probably by the end of this night would think he was a burglar.

"Hey, look at the time!" exclaimed Hugh. "Time to get the groom in place and us to change. Let's get moving!"

They loaded into the truck, with the gifts and the plants.

Arriving at Chuck's house, they hustled Brad again down to the beach where a firepit had been cooking food all day, a large canopy had been set up and decorated, a stage set up. The gifts joined others that were on a long table at the back. Chuck carefully arranged Brad's gifts to his bride to show to best effect. The envelopes they had been gifted he neatly lay on the table so that the places they came from could be seen. He noticed several other envelopes were waiting as well. Two women who were already at the other end of the table arranging gifts smiled at them.

"Such a handsome man!" exclaimed one older lady.

"Yes, but has he got proper manners? Will he take care of his wahini?" frowned the other.

"If these friends have done their job, he will," replied the first. They marched up to the house. Brad shook his head. "They were supposed to represent her relatives and are supposed to give you a hard time so you know to not misuse their cousin or daughter," explained Chuck. "They're harmless and have to act grumpy all night but most of them don't mean it." Three people were setting out feast food, digging up what had been cooking in the pit, setting out other dishes. One young man had set up a bar to the side. A band had set up on the stage. To one side of the canopy sat two high chairs. Brad was ceremoniously sat down in one and given a cold glass of some fruity drink. He sniffed it suspiciously but Chuck assured him there was no alcohol.

Promptly at 7, dancers came down the slope to the beach in grass skirts and leis leading the ladies' group, consisting of Chuck's wife, several bridesmaids, and Casey bringing up the rear. Brad thought he'd never see anything quite as welcome or half as lovely as Casey, her hair decked out with flowers, slim and lithe in her white dress, swaying as she walked towards him. Chuck's wife led her to Brad, placed her hand in his and smiled.

"Now to enjoy. Chuck is going to say grace and then we can begin eating and everything will unfold as it will."

There was a sound of sirens. Police cars stopped at the top of the hill and four officers charged down.

"Are you Brad Malcom?" demanded one.

"Yes, sir." The policemen looked around and must have realized they were interrupting a luau.

"Listen, sorry we need to bother you right now, but earlier today, a box was mailed to this household to you from the mainland. The post office scanner found traces of chemicals on the box. They alerted us and we took it apart very carefully. It had three things in it, one a low energy explosive device that would have done little more than spread indelible ink on everything within ten feet or so, similar to ones used at banks to catch robbers by drenching them in ink and making them very noticeable. There was also a Ziploc bag with some fabric in it with a note addressed to you and a cat mummy? Do you recognize this handwriting and do you have any idea who could have done this? It's a federal crime to send something like this through the mail."

Brad took the note. All it said was, "You can fly away but you can't hide. I'll see you both on Founder's Day." In the plastic bag was a quilt block. He looked at it, stunned.

Casey turned white. Brad's wife helped her sit down. "That cat is from Mike's store back home!" Casey exclaimed. "It's supposed to be in its' display case. How did it get here?"

The officer went on. "We thought maybe this was a prank from some friends on the mainland who doesn't realize you can't put this sort of stuff through the US mail?"

"Officer, Brad's a policeman on his honeymoon," replied Chuck. "Back home, he's working on a case where the victim is always marked with a quilt square." Numbly, Brad pulled out his ID and his badge and spoke. "Please contact my Sheriff back home, Erick Black. Homeland is helping with this and I have no idea how they all knew where we went. Casey, contact your mom," he handed her his phone and she texted rapidly. "We need to be sure they're OK."

An auntie came up to Casey. "That's a Cat and Mice square," she said. "I've not seen one of those in ages. It's made very well."

One officer went to call Erick; another took statements and were invited to stay to the feast. Being on duty, they couldn't but after speaking with Erick, Brad requested they Fedex the box block and the mummy to his home station; the cops conferred with their station and agreed to do so, leaving with the evidence.

The entire crowd of people stood looking shell-shocked. After a long pause, Chuck announced, "So, we know what Brad will be going home to but that's a week away and right now, we have a feast to eat and I for one, could use a mai tai.

This is still the traditional marriage ceremony and we are going to finish it up! Let tomorrow worry about tomorrow. Get the music going, start dancing and in an hour, we'll have the ceremony and do these best friends of mine right by us."

The drums began, the band joined in, the dancers danced. Casey sat very still holding Brad's hand. She was given a fruity drink as well, and when her text from her mom came back that all was well, she relaxed and they started to join in on the fun.

Chapter Nine

Mrs. Armstrong leaned back with a satisfied look on her face.

"There! All done. Your mom is so going to love this quilt."

Annie nodded. "And I could so use a walk right now."

"Where to today, chick?" laughed her grandma as she folded the quilt carefully, wrapped it in tissue paper, put it in a box she had gotten at the packing store, and sealed it up for the trip home. "With my friends' help, it's all done and now I think a walk to the pack and ship is in order." She finished addressing the box to herself.

"Grandma, mom said Brad and us are going to live at his farmlet. I went there once and it's pretty nice. Shouldn't we be mailing it there?"

"Oh, no, I want to properly wrap it and fetch it over to them at the delayed reception."

"The what?"

"Founder's Day, part of the celebration is the reception the kids never had. Our church ladies have got all the presents stored in the church basement, we're going to decorate the fellowship hall, put in the gifts, bring out the real wedding cake, and hold the reception for the family and friends. Then we'll all go out to see the fireworks."

"That's so cool. Are we getting the petting zoo back and everything?"

"No, just stuff in the basement. There's already going to be bouncy houses and the petting zoo set up for the celebration in the park. Mildred back home told me last night that they're already getting up the decorations and such. The sheriff and all those federal guys are all over it, making sure it's safe. Something about getting new intel or something. Half the time I can't understand what Mildred says when she gets excited."

"So we're walking to the mailing place?"

"Yeah, and I want an ice cream sundae to celebrate being done. The parlor is right next to the Pak and Ship."

"Sounds good." grinned Annie. "Where did the Aunts' go?"

"They still work, remember? Just us. I'll lock up. Oh, that must be the mailman." Mrs. Armstrong went over to the mail slot in the front door and picked up the mail.

"Now that's odd! There's a package here for us and it's from Maui."

"Mom must have sent us something!" declared Annie. "Open it!"

"Let me get a knife in the kitchen. It's sort of flat. Too small for t-shirts. Not really lumpy. I do like surprises."

Mrs. Armstrong got a sharp knife, slit open the package and spilled it out on the counter. There was a zipper bag. Inside it was fabric. Mrs. Armstrong's face started to go white.

"What is it?" asked Annie. She took it and her face fell.

"Oh, rats!" she declared. She pulled out a quilt block and a note fluttered to the floor.

She picked it up and read it out loud. "Grandma, it says, "See you at Founder's Day. Have a safe trip." What the devil? How did those creeps find us up here in Wisconsin?"

"That block is called Devil's Claw," muttered her grandma. "I'm going to call the Sheriff... don't handle that. Put it back in the bag. We are air shipping it to Erick the same time we're sending out your mom's quilt. And don't tell them, OK? This could ruin their honeymoon. We don't want them getting upset and coming home early."

Chapter Ten

"There!" exclaimed Suzanne to the ladies. "That's the second of Marie's quilts done. We can call her son and let her know to come in anytime he has available."

"Actually, I'm working on quilt number three from her, and the sheriff's deputy just dropped off quilt number four," answered Miriam. "Appears there's another son and this one is for him. They're so pretty. I just got it set up on the long arm. Odd how perfect they are, each one almost a mirror image of the other except for the middle."

"Not quite. See the square in the middle? She has a different family I each one. I think this one is Toby's because there isn't any lady or kids. This must be Liam's because there is his wife holding a baby silhouette."

"Then this one?"

"Marie sent in a silhouette of a man, wife, and two little ones to add to the middle blank block, so her other son must have a family."

"I wonder who the fifth quilt was supposed to be for, you know, the one that has been used in all those crimes?"

"Toby said it was Arthur's, the one who died in the war. Since the blocks were already cut out, she made them up but had no one to give it to and allowed him to sell the blocks online. Somehow, the criminal got them all, even though they sent them all over the place."

"It's a puzzle," said Lydia. "I'll mind the store in front while you quilt."

"Fine," beamed her boss. "It will be about two hours and then we'll be all set to binding it and they can all go home as soon as they are picked up."

"There goes the bell, I'd best be on my way out front," smiled Lydia, walking out.

Suzanne worked in silence for a few minutes. "Marie does such good work." she remarked.

Miriam nodded to her. "She does. I will be glad when Founder's Day is over. I have this feeling something is going to happen and I just want it over with; we usually love to come in and see the fireworks and the animals and enjoy the town a little bit but Bishop is thinking it might be safer to be home. He is considering not allowing those of us with jobs to come in that day for safety's sake. I am going to do my best but our Bishop is a cautious man."

"I do hope he doesn't," exclaimed Suzanne. "It' going to be busy in here and if we lose all our Amish helpers, it's going to be impossible to keep up. But you do what you need to do to be safe."

Miriam nodded, completed making the quilting kits she was cutting out, and then proceeded to bag them to add to the displays out front.

Chapter Eleven

Erick looked up.

"According to that tablet they deciphered, the next attack is on Founder's Day. It doesn't say where or what but we have to double our guard," he said to Troy.

"Shortly will have more feds here than locals," he replied. He continued working on his computer. "That last quilt block, the one that was sent to Brad, has it arrived yet?"

"Just came in," replied the dispatcher out front. She came in with the package and handed it to Erick.

"It's called Homeward Bound and it's not in the original quilt."

"Marvelous. He's branching out." grumped Troy. "Has anyone heard from Annie or Mrs. Armstrong?"

"There was another envelope from them, oddly." replied the dispatcher. "It's from Mrs. Armstrong."

"That's not good." He opened it. "She says this arrived at her sister's house yesterday and she sent it to me; she says it's called Devil's Claw. Suzanne made a quilt with this block a few years ago."

"It's not in the original quilt either."

"He wanted us to know he knows where they went. How on earth did he find them?" demanded Jim.

"That's irrelevant," Ali answered. "When are they due back?"

"Brad is due middle of the next week. They're taking two days to move into the new place and he'll be on duty for Founder's Day, like the rest of us," replied his dispatcher from the front. She'd left the door open, knowing hr boss would keep talking to her. "I'm not sure but Mrs. Armstrong is due home before that."

"I'm going to call her and find out if she told Casey about this."

Troy spoke up. "Did we find out where the rest of the decals are from? Any leads there?" He ran his fingers through his hair and looked harassed. "What are we missing?"

"Let's go over it all again," replied Jim Alia. "We're getting close. There has to be one more piece we're missing." He went to the whiteboard and looked at everything hanging on it. He moved a few things over to add to the list written there.

"OK, we know Marie Clamons made the blocks. We're also pretty sure she didn't know they were being used in the crimes." he checked that off.

"We know she had 4 sons and a half son. Arthur, the oldest, died in the war. He's out of the running. Troy, the half son, is here, an agent. Toby is with her and has had alibis for everything. Matthew Solomon, a son, isn't speaking to her. He's in Chicago mostly. Liam is here in town, a pharmacist. Any other relatives, friends, anything? Somehow, three of the brothers have a joint apartment that does not seem to be getting used regularly over in Columbus."

"There's Toby's friend Kevin Daniels, the computer whiz. Toby has a lot of workmates who think the world of them, they're all nurses, doctors, therapists, you know, medical types. They all check out as not having known him much before he came here. Dr. Michaels knew them in the war; they saved his life, he saved theirs. Comrades in arms? His alibis check out." said Jed.

"We know Marie's house was sold after a painful divorce leaving her destitute; we know her sons were taken away from her, except Toby. He surprised everyone by surviving, thriving, and making something of himself to the point that he bought back his mom's house with a combination of GI bill and help from his pharmacist brother, who is by all accounts, somewhat of a tightwad. We know Toby was the channel through which the blocks were sold, but they were sold widely. The link between seller and buyer was Paypal driven, an Etsy account. We have control of that now. These last two blocks that occurred in Maui and Wisconsin were not made by Marie."

"How do we know that?" asked Troy.

"Different fabric, different sewing machine, different style of stitches. I've had both our local expert and another expert look at them and do a comparison so these were not made by her," replied Alli.

"So is our guy branching out?"

"Must be. What else have we got?" asked Jim.

"The tablet had a list of everything that has happened so far up until the tablet was lost except the Maui and the Wisconsin blocks seems he didn't know about the wedding or trips until midway and then, of course, didn't have the tablet to keep up. The tablet listed the place, person, time in a spreadsheet. We know he's methodical. We know he's organized. The last entries, that happened after the tablet was found, are not filled in because the tablet is not in his possession." replied Erick.

"And that must be making him miserable if he truly is obsessive," added Ally. "His uncontrollable, recurring insistence on control and exactness will force him to do things exactly the same way each time. OCD folks have definite patterns and we almost had this one until the last two blocks. They break the pattern which makes me think he is not the head of the group, the one who sent these last blocks. He is either a copycat or someone is trying to throw us off the trail." Erick had gone over to the wall display of the thumbprints of the quilts. He studied it, then went to the quilt file and pulled out the last two.

"I have seen this fabric before. I don't know where."

"Quilt shop locally has over 3000 bolts in stock," said Alli. "Could have come from there. It's not discount fabric, too heavy, too pretty. It's got to be from a quilt shop. It's fabric a quilter would appreciate. Notice the blocks aren't paper pieced; the points aren't as sharp," she turned the fabric piece over. "And see these little tiny pieces of paper? She used thangles, a sort of pattern to make triangles with, to get them accurate enough for this pattern."

"Didn't know you did quilts," said Erick.

"My grandma taught me. Haven't done one in years. It's relaxing and enjoyable to see it all come together. Our perp used larger stitches to put it together. All of Marie's are regular lengths; these are larger as if this person knows she might have to tear a line out so made the stitches easier to do that with a seam ripper. My conclusion is that I'd agree with whomever the experts were; this is not Marie's work."

"Great!" exclaimed Jim. "Where does that lead us?"

"The perp is now improvising. He's bending to meet the circumstances. He is moving from his MO, so I am thinking he's not obsessive. He's in more of a revenge state of mind. It has to be someone who knew what Marie went through, and Toby, someone close to them."

"We need to find out who their friends were back then, who would hold a grudge after all these years."

"And I still think we are dealing with more than one person. Someone local would know of the change in Brad's itinerary, for instance. Who knows the Armstrong's well?" asked Erick.

"Matt Armstrong would know," said Jed. "I'll go have a visit and see what he says."

Jim nodded. "How are we going at getting in touch with the decal people?"

"Mayor told me that the company they use is called Majestic Decals. They can make stuff up to eight feet across. He gave me contact info and then took me to where they keep the decals in storage for reuse and two are missing, the rest are accounted for. Two of them we found."

"Grand! Alli?"

"I've got three VM's into them and one email. No reply. They're up in Euclid."

"Get in touch with Euclid and see if they can pay a call, get the info and send it here. Could be they are just too busy to reply," said Jim.

"Troy, Go get Toby and Liam and bring them in for questioning. Becky, have we got contact info on Matthew?"

"Now, you're yelling through the door, too?" Becky snorted in disgust from the front. "Yeah, I have his last known address."

"Have Franklin county go get him and send a deputy to bring him back here."

"I don't think you have to," replied Troy. "I saw him with Liam not an hour ago driving that little orange bug out of town. Also saw the pastor's wife driving the same make, model, and year heading after them."

"What's the Pastor's wife got to do with it?" asked Erick.

"Don't know. Just telling what I saw. If I see Matthew, I'll bring him in as well." Troy stood up.

"OK, rest of you, you have your assignments, be careful out there, keep your eyes open. We have to catch this guy before this weekend. Founder's Day starts next weekend. I want him safely behind bars so these folks can enjoy the celebration. They haven't had a normal day since last Founder's Day."

"Oh, I don't know," smiled Erick. "Last Founder's Day, three Amish on Rumspringa and four town fellas got bombed and raced their buggies down the Main street of town right at dawn, figuring not to be caught. Upset lots of folks. And then my wife and the ladies got caught as they were yarn bombing the gazebo in the park, making the Memorial Band from the High School all upset, since they yarn bombed in red, white and blue and the band is in the school colors of purple and gold, and the uniforms clashed. I almost had to arrest six old ladies, my wife, and her cronies for defacing public property with yarn...and as I recall, we had four lost kids, three shoplifting incidents. I don't know, those were the good old days...when our worst problems were old ladies with knitting needles and crochet hooks and Amish buggies." He shook his head.

"Let's get back to them, shall we?" laughed Jim. "It's a place I'd like to visit when it wasn't being blown up. OK, everybody, get going."

Chapter Twelve

Two days later, Mrs. Armstrong and Annie reported to the Sheriff's office that they had arrived safely. Mrs. Armstrong gave him her account of the quilt block once more. He called her son Matthew Armstrong to take her home and sent a deputy with her to be sure she got there safely. While they waited, Annie started chattering to the Sheriff.

"Wisconsin is nice, Sheriff Black," said Annie. "We got a quilt done for mom and Brad and my aunts cook better than Ricci! I wanted to bring back some lasagna but we couldn't back it right to do it, but we got the recipe."

"And you will invite us all over when you make it, right?" smiled Alli. It was difficult to be serious around the bubbly middle schooler.

"Might have to double the recipe to do that but we can, right Grandma?"

"Tell you what, let's get through Founder's Day and we'll have a celebration. Your mom and new dad need to get all moved in and I'm on the Garden Club committee. Starting tomorrow, I'll be busting my back with the other ladies decorating. We're determined to put all this horrible stuff behind us and have the best celebration ever. It's going to be really busy for a few days. This is the year we hang decals and have the barn celebration and I don't know if anyone took over for poor Melissa?" The sheriff shook his head. Grandma went on, nodding back. "When it all calms down, we'll have them all over for our own celebration. Here's your uncle, let's go and let them get back to work," smiled her grandma. They left with him, Annie still chattering about the trip.

"She's a sweet kid," remarked Alli.

"She's well raised, too," answered Erick. "Mayor said his wife and the Garden committee have ordered in some decals and they ought to arrive shortly. They stayed completely away from the normal colors and went with things in red, white, and blue. They had to get six of them to add to what they have and they're going to be putting them up tomorrow. The farmers have painted that end of their barns."

"Not the whole barn?" asked Jim.

"Most of them didn't need it. We have good folk here who keep things up and they're ready for the drive through the country to be a pretty one. They're each offering refreshments and something a little different for folks to see; Bill Williams has a beef herd and will have a couple of calves where folks can pet them, and Jim Samuels has a dairy farm and will be showing folks the milk house, Trevor Frederick has an organic grain farm, well, you get the idea. The tour is going to take all of the afternoons, so the first celebration is Saturday at 10 in the park at the gazebo. The High school band is playing as is the Memorial band which is sort of like the alumni of the high school band, and the mayor is speaking, they're having a balloon launch; everyone present gets a balloon, they have messages on them requesting they be sent back so we can see which went the furthest and people can win based on who's come back from the farthest away. We have the petting zoo and bouncy houses and the just the people from town reception in the basement of the church. They are vendors and games and contests for the prettiest garden; we have six sets of judges judging various things from a cake contest to a flower slow; all the stores have sidewalk sales or inside sales. We already know of nine buses of people coming in just for the quilt show. Oh, and there's a quilt raffle. Sunday is the parade and more of the barn tour and local bands and musicians are competing all day in the gazebo; there are pony rides and a miniature train for the preschoolers made of barrels and for gosh sake, it's a huge deal here. We're honoring the Founder's and I don't think anyone even knows their names when they get here but by the time they leave, they will. I need fifty more men to police it all. I don't know what's been planned to disrupt it all but this maniac has already killed two people and blown up the library. What are we going to do? You guys at fed know crowd control and protection and stuff, what haven't I covered to make us safe? I don't want to lose anyone else. The baby from the explosion's funeral nearly killed me, so sad."

Jim put his hand on the older lawman's shoulder. "It's rough. Let's go over your plans again. Let's see what needs moved around or augmented. In the meantime, everyone's out gathering more info. Let's hope we're near to the end of it. Founder's Day is the last thing listed. What we don't know. When we do. It has to happen Sunday, the actual day, April 25. Just like an algebra problem, we ought to be able to extrapolate the size and place once we figure the pattern."

"I think the last two blocks can be eliminated as just bravado," said Alli. "Sort of like, we see you, you can't run from me, I'm going to get you type of nonsense. They don't fit. There are just two establishments in town that look like they have anything to do with the perp."

Jim jerked around. "What?"

"Look at it. Marie Clamons and her family's troubles are the middle of it. Sort of like a web out. Several people hurt her and her children badly; the bank who took the house, the teacher who bought it, the ex whose already dead, the school where her child was teased. Look at the quilt she made and what we have. The middle was her family disintegrating. All the places she was surrounded by when her kids were growing up, all the buildings have been hit. The original courthouse was blown to bits-that's where the official auction was held. I don't think the library was the target there, it was ancillary to blowing the courthouse to Kingdom come. The other places-remember how they were held together by the graffiti that looked like quilting lines? The entire town was in her quilt and they have all been attacked in some way. The descendants of the people who hurt her were all hit; Brad's dad had to hold the auction. His son was kidnapped and has been stalked, his fiancé kidnapped. David Hershberger's father bought her beloved sewing machine-his son was kidnapped. Miriam worked for Suzanne, the daughter of the lady who had originally arranged for Marie's quilt to be shown to the museum who bought it. Suzanne's son was attacked but fought it off. Looking at the quilt and looking at the history Brad and the Mayor provided for us, my best guess for an attack is going to be the present courthouse where all the records are kept. The records of the embarrassment of losing their home. It's all to do with that one family."

"The courthouse houses the little town museum on the first floor. It's always open for folks to go through and see the displays about the original buildings and such;" muttered Erick. "The rest of the building is closed. There's a couple of ladies from the flower club who are always there to show folks around and be sure nothing happens to the displays. The records are all on microfiche in the basement. We haven't gotten them all put on the computer yet. I mean, a lot of them are from the early 1800s, and it just didn't seem too pressing. We've been having interns do them over the summers."

"The other place to hit would be the gazebo. It's been there in one form or another since 1856. Rebuilt when needed, always there. And it's the site of the marriage of Jack and Marie. It seems sensible that the perp would want it blown away."

"That makes sense too."

"Our third possible but maybe improbable is the paint factory. Marie went to work there and ended up with cancer. The old one and the old owner is long gone. The new paint factory seems to have not been considered as a target. I can't figure out why and it's bothering me big time."

"My bigger question is how are they going to do it?" asked Jim.

"Well, they used plastic explosives before, so they know how to do it.," she replied.

"As soon as Troy gets back with all the Clamon's men, we're separating them and starting questioning. And I'm calling in the bomb squad to go over the museum and the gazebo with fine-tooth combs. The celebration is next week." Erick said with finality. "We are going to get to the bottom of this."

"I don't think you'll find anything yet, and we don't want to tip our hand to any of them, Troy included," remarked Alli. "Let's have the bomb squad get here maybe the day before. We still don't have the head of this beast. There has got to be someone else leading it, but who else in town would care if Marie is avenged? Is it actually about revenge?”

“We haven’t seen any other motives,” replied her boss. “Revenge is one of the oldest motives we’ve seen.”

Shaking her head, she returned to the historical records. “Is there anyone we can ask about the situation when Marie was divorced?”

Erick thought a moment. “I’d say Mildred and Sophia, but heaven help me for suggesting that. Those two old biddies are best friends with every garden club and yarn lady in town, including my wife and Marie. I can just feel cold suppers coming on for weeks if wife knows we’ve questioned them.”

“Let me do it,” said Alli. “I’m fairly good with little old ladies.”

“Tell you what, take Jed with you. He’s a nephew to Sophia. And I suggest you stop at the bakery and take them both a box of muffins. They love them and are on fixed incomes so a treat helps.” Erick said.

Alli nodded. She and Jed left.

Jim shook his head. “I wonder if they will hit the new paint factory. On one hand, it enabled Marie to make enough money to raise her boy without support from her ex. On the other hand, it could have been the cause of her cancer.”

“The factory doesn’t match the pattern,” replied Erick.

“Excuse me?”

“They aren’t on Main street, where everyone saw Marie’s shameful humiliation.”

"That's true." Jim nodded.

"Erick, I'll take Troy, I know how to talk to feds and I'll take Matthew if they find him for the interview. You take Liam and Toby, they know you from town. Here's a list of suggested questions Alli made up to help. We're taping it all and she'll review it."

"You seem to depend on her a bunch."

"She's one of the best forensics we've got. She can find patterns and nuances everyone else misses. If we get anything slightly incriminating, we'll know at once."

Chapter Thirteen

"I really hate leaving Maui," sighed Casey as she packed. "It's been so peaceful, mostly. Getting back to the grind of to work by 7:33 is going to hard to get back to after sleeping in for two weeks cuddling. Everyone has been so nice, and your friend Chuck and his wife are the best."

"Yes, they are. I told them they could fly out and visit us on the farm once the little one's born and Chuck thought it might be nice to show her his old stomping grounds. "Her husband kept folding his clothes. "I can't believe all the presents from total strangers. I had no idea we'd be gifted like this. That luau was fantastic."

"Well, don't look now but we still have our wedding reception back home to go to."

"Really?"

"Mom texted me and said they're having it afternoon Sunday of Founder's Day in the church basement. The cake will be set up, the present there to be opened, well-wishers doing the hugging thing, and then we all recess up to the street for square dancing and such. They're expecting at least all the relatives, friends, and such to drop by. It's to last two hours. It's at 7 so most the tourists and hopefully all the danger will be over by then, and you ought to be off duty, Lord willing.

You have All day Saturday and Sunday 7 to 5, right?" Brad nodded as he packed.

"From your mouth to God's ears," he murmured as he closed his suitcase. "You about done?"

"Yes, all our stuff but these are in the pick-up and after lunch on the deck, Chuck's taking us to the airport and we go out with him at 2. I am going to miss them so."

"Let me carry it down. It's a long flight home."

"I know." Her cell went off and she checked the text. "Mom and Annie are deep into the prep for Founder's Day and midterms for Annie. She is hating her algebra class."

"She does ok in it, though?"

"Yeah, she has a solid B but everything else is an A and she's just upset her GPA is not 4.0 like last year."

"Won't keep her out of college."

"I know. But she's an overachiever."

"Like her mom," Brad said as he hugged Casey. "I can't wait to get home, suddenly, sort of homesick for Rutherford."

"For the dog?"

"Oh, among other things. The spring flowers will be up, and there's this part of the woods that's thick with dogwoods and trillium, wood sorrel, spring beauties, and violets and I can't wait to take you there for a picnic. The forsythia ought to be blooming out back by our yard swing and I guess after two weeks in paradise, there's no place like home." He kissed her. "Let me get the suitcases to the truck." He headed out. She took a last look around the room, then went out to the deck to take a picture of the ocean, the flowers along the beach and the palms, then followed him out.

Chuck and Candy met them in the kitchen with plates of island delicacies.

They all went out back to eat, enjoy the ocean breezes, and say goodbyes. The men finished quickly and went out to talk by the truck, while the ladies spent a few minutes cleaning up and chatting.

"I've called in a few favors about your flights," started Chuck. "They're checking every flight for problems but it looks good. My bird's been gone over with a fine-tooth comb and is being watched. Even the cops have come out to see us off, so we probably best be going."

Brad nodded. "I really appreciate all you've done to make this a great honeymoon."

"Casey's a wonderful woman," Chuck said. "I think we both lucked out. You'll be safe getting home from here."

"We're actually being picked up at the airport by the Sheriff himself in a police van. I suspect we'll be secure. Erick's had our place checked over and is checking it again before we move in. All our boxes and such have been wanded going on to the flight at this end and will be checked at that end. I don't see how we could do much more to ensure a safe homecoming."

"You let us know when you get there, you hear me?" said Chuck. He hugged Brad. "Here come the ladies."

A few minutes earlier, back in the house, the ladies had said goodbye over cleaning up the dinner in the kitchen and on deck. As they had carried in plates, they talked about the trip.

"It won't feel the same without you here, now," stated Candy. "I've gotten used to having you to visit. It's been lovely."

"Well, thank you for letting us use your home. You be sure to send me pictures of that baby when she comes." smiled Casey. "I bet she's going to be gorgeous."

"I hope so. Maybe we can come out and see snow after she's born. I've never seen it much. I was born and raised in the south and then we moved here when I was a teen and snow just isn't a big thing."

"You come out and stay with us anytime. We'll show you how to ice skate and sled and snowshoe. It will be grand."

"Well, Chuck grew up in Montana, so he's seen drifts higher than the house," answered Candy. Sher paused. "You let me know when they catch that bad guy they've been chasing. From what Brad said, he's done a lot of damage."

"He has. It's a worry. Brad is going to leave Rutherford with us whenever he has to be away and we're home alone, as he calls it. But we're so far out in the country surrounded by Amish, I can't imagine anyone would bother us. Still good to know we're protected. And I've got a CCW too, and a good little pistol if it comes to that. I pray it doesn't."

"Well, Chuck will get you to the mainland. Then you'll be on commercial flights."

"I can't believe we came with two suitcases and are leaving with, my land, how many boxes? Live trees and plants and chimes and it's all been so much. I don't know how to thank you enough for all you've done and arranged. And mailing them all home yesterday was a great idea. I can't wait to hang those chimes in my yard and put the quilt on our bed. You be sure to thank all those ladies for me? I feel so overwhelmed by their generosity and their acceptance they showed us. The luau was incredible. Well, except for the cops. And the box and the mummy. But the love was all there."

"I'll tell them and here, I made you a little album: we all took pictures at the luau and put them together for you and all the ladies' names and addresses are in the back. If you get time, drop them a line. And you can thank me by getting home safe and sending me a message when you get there and maybe some pictures of the town? I'd love to see it."

"I can do that, sure. Let me help with the dishes?"

"No, Chuck and Brad are waiting by the truck. You've got a plane to catch." The two ladies hugged. "I feel like I got the sister I never had," said Candy. "You take care."

"You too," said Casey. "Guess we go now." They went out and Casey got in the truck cab, as did the men. The drive to the island airport seemed ever so short. Chuck's plane had been gone over, packed, and pre-flighted. They loaded up, taxied off, and were soon in the air.

Chapter Fourteen

Lizbeth Primo went to the courthouse Tuesday with three lovely floral arrangements, intended for the Mayor's office, the front gift shop of the historical museum, and the museum desk in the second room. They were just the right size for each place, not too much or too little, showing her refinement.

"These are lovely, gushed the receptionist. Let's set them in place, shall we? We can replace the silk flowers here on this little table outside the office with this live flower arrangement and let me take you into the museum to set these up. It's so kind of you to arrange for these."

"They're just from our garden," smiled Lizbeth. "I do love flowers. I've put them in a weakened soda solution so they ought to be good well into next week. I can come back for the vases then. They belong to the church supplies."

"Well, we appreciate it. Did you see how nice the park looks?"

"Oh" laughed the pastor's wife. "Yes, but the yarn bombing on the gazebo pillars, let's just say certain senior ladies have outdone themselves. The sequins knotted into the yarn are," she paused. "Festive."

"Bright as politician's dentures, you ask me. Anyway, the flower clubs divided up the park and are vying with their assigned beds to have them just perfect, knowing the one best voted gets a trophy this year. It was nice of the folks on the committee to get trophies. Usually, we have ribbons but really, they are going all out to make this year the best festival yet." The ladies completed setting up the flowers.

"The janitor did a good job getting this all dusted and clean," remarked Lizbeth. "I don't see any fingerprints in the glass cases or anything. Excellent."

"Yes, our new janitor is a whiz. Can't find any fault in his diligence, unlike the last two that I always had to fuss at to get things right. This man is almost obsessive about it being clean. Thank you so much for introducing him to us."
Lizbeth nodded.

"I think it speaks well for our town to have it so nice." She looked around. "I do hope the tours go well."

"They should if hard work can make it happen. And we've advertised in the state magazine and online as well. The farmers are coming up with all sorts of grand things to do on the barn tour and we have everyone pitching in."

"Well, it is the biggest fundraiser for the merchants of the year. One of them told me it balances their books out through Christmas in good years. What with all the bad things that have been happening, we all worried it would be called off or at least delayed. One year we delayed it and ran up against bigger towns with huge festivals and they didn't do well at all. Having ours be one of the first in the entire state has helped immensely with the local economy."

"You're right about that. Well, thank you again," said the receptionist, locking the doors to the museum behind them.

"Did I hear right that some of the factories will be giving tours?"

"Well, you know the Amish furniture factory always does that, but it appears the mill and the paint factory are going to be opening their doors as well. They're putting out some souvenirs, you know pens and yardsticks, litter bags, that sort of thing, and refreshments on-site and guest's books to see what it does for them as well. All of it is being printed up in things to do type bulletin. I guess it's worrying Erick pretty badly. He feels his men are being spread too thin to watch everything. I hear he's having help in from the surrounding townships. I do hope they aren't needed."

"Well, let's hope not," replied Lizbeth. "I need to go be certain the church is ready for prayer meeting."

"We'll see you there," smiled the receptionist.

Chapter Fifteen

Erick and Jim met Troy followed by all the living Clamons men he'd gathered up.

"This is a formality at this point," started Erick. "But we need to pick your brains. This is Jim Alia from Homeland Security, that's Alli Stewart, also Homeland. Troy you already know."

"Where's Brad?" asked Toby. "I thought he was going to be back Monday."

"He is, but he has a couple of days off yet that he's using to move into his new place with his bride. He's going to be here Thursday. Now, Troy, you and Matthew go back to the first room on the left, Toby and Liam, you follow me."

"Do I need my lawyer?" asked Toby.

"You're not being accused of anything. We're trying to see if you could possibly know something that could help us with the case. I don't think you'll incriminate yourselves. If you feel you want a lawyer and have one, you could ask them in. We're not taking your cell phones or anything but do ask you to turn them off until we're done and keep them face down on the table. We're actually going to ask each of you pretty much the same questions. Your choice about calling the lawyer. Right now, we're looking for leads."

The four men shortly found themselves in different rooms of the station. Toby sat in the visitation room for the small jail; Liam was in the first interview room; Matthew was in room two, and Troy was in an office. Alli had cameras set up in all four rooms, the conversations were being recorded, and she was watching all four interviews at once on her computer. She asked the receptionist not to allow anyone in the room or any calls until they were done.

Erick decided to talk to Toby first. He brought his clipboard, a can of soda for himself and Toby, and went in.

"Hey, Toby, I'd like to keep this as short as we can because I know we're all busy. You like cola? " Without letting him answer, he opened it and set it in front of him. "Here, it should be good and cold, just got it out of the fridge. I have to do the official demographic stuff first, then I'll get to the actual case questions, OK?"

"How long is this going to take? I usually check on mom and have a nap before I head in for the afternoon shift."

"When's work?"

"I have to be there at 3."

"OK, it's 10, so let's try to get this done in the next couple hours and you can be on your way."

Toby nodded.

"Full name?"

"Tobias Seth Clamons."

"Date of Birth?" The sheriff went through the usual address, email, phone numbers, employment demographics, studiously writing them down. Finally, he said, "Toby, we have your list of alibi's for all the dates of all the incidents, but I wanted to know if you recall anything about those particular dates that may have stuck out for you?"

"What do you mean, exactly?" asked Toby.

"There's this niggling kind of thing in my head that the dates mean something, they're spaced so strangely as if they were reaching a conclusion. We have all those quilt blocks your mom made that you sent out to buyers, and they all went everywhere it seems. But the spacing of the crimes seems sort of methodical as if tied to some other occurrence. Would you have any ideas on that?" Toby considered and then spoke slowly.

"Well, actually, I have sort of thought about that, just the dates you had me lookup. I know it seems funny, and there's probably nothing to it, but, you know, it's odd. I made a sort of chart up about it. I've got it on my phone. Here, let me get it." He strummed down through his phone.

"Here it is. See, the first thing that happened, the first date I needed an alibi for? That was my mom and dad's wedding anniversary. The next one was Arthur's birthday. And the next one I don't know but the one after that was my birthday, and the next Liam's. I don't know about the next one either. But two others occurred on Troy and Matthew's birthdays. And one happened the day our house was taken away. It's almost as if they knew the important events of my family and picked them." The sheriff looked surprised, looked at the chart, and pointed.

"Which was that?"

"When the old courthouse building blew up. It was the same day we lost our house." Erick considered.

"Seems appropriate, doesn't it?"

"It's never right to hurt people like that but if I was out looking for revenge for a sorry childhood, it would make sense. I'm not but still."

"What other dates seemed coincidental?" asked the Sheriff. "And can you send that list to me?"

"Sure. Where do I send it?" He private messaged the chart and the sheriff added the email address for Alli to it. "The other two dates are the day dad got remarried and the day my half-sister ran off. She was pregnant and we never saw her again."

"You have a half-sister?"

"No one talks about her." The sheriff looked thoughtful.

"You know, Casey is a social worker and she showed me a thing they use sometimes to keep things organized. She calls it a genogram. It's like a family tree. Maybe we need to have you do one of those. Let me just go get some blank paper instead of these forms and I'll do that. Seems there's more to your family than I expected."

The Sheriff left the room, got some printer paper in legal size, and put it on a clipboard. He picked up a handful of sharpie markers and slipped them into his pocket. He then went in to see Liam.

After the initial demographics and assurances that he wasn't under suspicion, he asked Liam, "Did you have any other siblings besides Toby, Arthur, Matthew, and Troy?"

"Well, actually, now that you bring it up, we had a sister, actually she joined mom and me once Jack married her. She belonged to Jack I think, I was, I don't know, ten or so and she was just there when we arrived. She was older and only stayed a little while. I think she got pregnant or something, anyway, the first step-mom sent her away and I never saw her again I don't recall her name, I think it was a Biblical name, Rebecca? Bess? Beth? I really don't recall. Marie might remember. I haven't thought about her in years."

"Listen," said the Sheriff. "I want to draw a sort of family tree so I can keep all these folks straight. This square is your dad, Jack Clamons. This circle is your stepmom, Marie Clamons, and this is your mom, Sheila Clamons, and he had a third wife, any idea who she was?"

"No, I never met her that I recall. I left when dad lost custody. I stayed with Marie for almost a year, dad got remarried and I joined the military with Arthur."

"That's fine, I'm going to have each of you guys help me with this, someone will remember. Now you had a dad other than Jack, what was his name?"

"My birth dad was Allen Peters. He's deceased. Mom met Jack after dad passed from a car accident. Jack adopted me at mom's insistence. I never did get along with him." The sheriff carefully drew them in.

"Now let's draw lines down for each of you guys. Arthur belonged to which mom?"

"Arthur was Jack and Marie's first."

"You know his birthday?"

"March 10."

"Ok, where does Troy go?" One by one, they added the brothers. Liam seemed to know everyone's birthdays.

"That's going to help, I think. Now is there a reason why you, Matt, and Troy have an apartment in Columbus?" Liam jerked back and looked surprised.

"I don't have an apartment in Columbus." The sheriff looked surprised.

"I have a copy of a lease for you three for Apartment 3-D, 216 Sullivan Street, Columbus. Mail goes there addressed to all of you and the landlord says he has seen each of you there at different times."

"Who's the landlord?" demanded Liam. "All I have is a house here and now a car and the pharmacy business. I don't go to Columbus unless there's something Marti needs." He looked at the lease appearing baffled. "And I didn't know where Matthew was until last summer and this is dated three years ago. I was still working for Kroger's pharmacy over in Mansfield back then and Marti and I were just dating. If I was paying for an apartment, I'd know."

"Umm," said the Sheriff. "OK, the landlord said it was paid by money order like clockwork every 30th of the month, one day or so early each time and has been no problem. We've been there; there's furniture and food and everything in it and it looks lived in."

"Someone's using my name. That's identity theft."
Liam was getting irate.

"Don't worry, it just seemed like an odd thing. That's
why I brought it up, we're trying to clear some stuff up so we
can go forward with what is actually important to this case,
and you're right, here's the landlord's name and contact info
so you can go clear up why your name's on the lease. It just
looks suspicious, that's all. You three guys sharing an
apartment that had received some of the packages of quilt
blocks, well, that just looks suspicious."

"Quilt blocks? I thought you said they'd gone out all
over?"

"Yes, but they got redirected each time back to this
place."

"I want my lawyer here right now and I'm not saying
another thing. In fact, I'm leaving right now!" declared Liam.
"Your insinuations are insulting and flagrantly illegal."

"How so?"

"You're accusing me of something I didn't do."

"Well, that's not illegal exactly, but I can see it would
be aggravating. Tell you what, I'm going to go have the other
guys work on the family tree. Why don't you sit here and call
your lawyer and I'll get back to you." The sheriff stood up,
gathered his paperwork, and went back to Toby.

"OK, I stopped in to talk to Liam so he wouldn't think
I'd forgotten him and see if he could help us a bit. Here's what
he said. Now, where would you think the older half-sister
went?"

"Dad was married to another lady before Mom and I think that's where she came from. Her name was Rebecca Elizabeth Peters. She left when she was let's see, 15, I think, about the same age as Troy. The boys were already over there. I think I may have seen her once but I was ten or so. Mom told me this girl had gotten pregnant and they sent her away to have the baby and give it up for adoption and she never returned. They did that back then. I don't know her birthday, but Liam has all ours right, yes, and the anniversary of the divorce. I remember the day our house was auctioned and it was over here, Jack had already taken them all away, and me and mom were alone. He came for the auction and stood across the street watching, but he never came over to see us."

"And the sale date corresponded to the explosion date?"

"Yes."

"What's the next big thing that happened?"

Toby paused. "The Friday of Founder's Day is the day they were all given to my aunt and mom never saw them afterward. I remember she cried all weekend and we didn't go until Sunday to see the parade. I remember she gave me a balloon from the garden ladies and we launched them all and I remember how pretty they all were when we all let them go flying away, all those colors against a clear spring day sky, the picture is so vivid of all those balloons making polka dots as they rose. And then mom and I walked home to the apartment over the grocery store and had hots dogs and pork and beans to eat because the food from the vendors was too expensive. We had a candy bar we split for dessert. I didn't get candy much back then. I remember I'd go trick or treating and mom would ration it all out over the next months until Christmas or later; she kept it in the freezer and this was the last of it because we didn't have money for even a lollipop. And mom cried because for the first time in years she hadn't been able to help with the flowers at the festival. She'd always been in the flower show with the other garden ladies. The day before she had sold my quilt top the woman from the museum and she had that money now. She didn't keep it in the bank. Monday, she went down to the dentist and gave it to him and I got my braces. It wasn't a good time."

"I suspect not," replied the Sheriff. "Didn't you tell me Troy came to visit sometimes?"

"He came the summer after that for a few weeks. He was sort of smart-alecky back then and dad had had it and sent him to mom to live poor for a while so he'd respect dad. I don't think it worked. He took a shine to my mother and wished she'd been his mom. Liam visited us too for a few months when his mom left dad. I don't think he ever went back."

"Did you know that Liam, Troy, and Matthew have an apartment together in Columbus?"

"Why?"

"I was hoping you'd be able to tell me. See, we have this lease that showed up in our wandering around getting information and can't reconcile why they'd have it. I'll see if Matt or Troy can shine any light on it." He showed the lease to Toby.

"I'll be darned. Liam is so tight I can't imagine why he'd want another place to pay for."

"True," said the Sheriff. "Well, I promised you two hours and we're just about up., Anything else you can think of, you give me a call, all right?"

"I'll be sure to Sheriff. I want this settled as soon as we can. It's fretting mom pretty fierce and I'd like her to not have to worry about it anymore."

"Can you ask her if she knows anything about the stepsister?"

"If she's not too tired when I get back to the house. I'll see you around, Sheriff."

"Be safe," answered the Sheriff.

Erick walked into the office where Alli was waiting and gave her the genogram. She studied it a moment.

"I'll be darned. A woman involved as well. I don't think Toby has any idea what's going on."

"How did the other interviews go?"

"We'll review them all together later, one after the other when the others get back. One thing is sure, we can't have Troy working on this case anymore. There are too many holes. Still, I don't want to show our hand."

Erick nodded. "I can see that. Looks like Jim's leaning on him pretty hard."

"He was harder on Mathew and Matt's going to be our guest overnight while we check out his alibi's."

"OK. I'll get him booked in. He lawyered up yet?"

"Not that I know of. He's making some calls."

Chapter Sixteen

Erick met Casey and Brad at the airport. He was driving his own pick-up and arrived in time to see the plane land. He went inside and waited.

"You said to bring the pick-up and wasn't certain why?" asked the Sheriff.

"We got some wedding gifts and didn't think they'd fit in the squad car," replied Brad, who looked suntanned, rested, and suddenly really young to Erick. He gave himself a mental kick and reminded himself once, he and his wife had just come back from their honeymoon and looked every bit as young, in love and vulnerable as his sidekick was now. Brad held Casey's hand, she leaned against him, *clearly besotted*, he thought to himself. *People ought to be able to go away for a year until they've had one really good fight to temper the early foolishness. Still, it's good to see him at peace and happy again.*

"Gifts? Oh, that's good. Hey, Casey," he gave her a hug.

They walked to baggage claims and got the two suitcases. Then they went to the receiving office where sat two luggage carriers full of boxes.

"Mr. Malcom? Do you have your mailing slips?" asked the clerk with a smile.

"Yes, sir," Brad replied, taking a folded up long list out of his pocket. Erick began to get a queasy feeling in his stomach.

"These are all yours?" gasped Erick. "Do I see green poking out of one of those, no, two of those, no, three of those boxes? Did you at least leave the islands intact?"

Casey laughed. "And I did not shop for all this. They had an island shower for us. It was grand. I wish you could have been at the luau, well, except for the cops and the mummy and all. Let's load up and we can talk about it on the way home." she smiled. "Doesn't home sound like a lovely word? I am so looking forward to peace and quiet and settling in before I go back to work Monday. I want to plant my flowers and put the quilt on our bed and just cook on my own stove which I haven't seen yet. The peace and quiet of the country after the excitement of the islands. We do have a stove in the kitchen now, Brad?"

Brad completed signing for the boxes and nodded. "Yep, it was delivered last Tuesday. I had help choosing a good one. Erick, if you can push that one, I can push this one."

Erick stood there. He looked from Casey to Brad and back. Brad put his finger to his lips and nodded. Erick took a deep breath.

"Excuse me, Mr. Malcom." announced the clerk. "We have to have our personnel push them while in the terminal. Regulations. Pete, Sam, take these out front please." Two men, one burly, one tall and thin, came out of the back and took control of the carriers, pushing them towards the front of the terminal.

Brad asked, "Erick, where's the pick-up?"

"It's in the lane out front for loading. I'll go get the tailgate down." He trotted off. Brad and Casey followed at a little slower pace, watching the baggage handlers as they pushed the carriers through the crowds with surety and safety, missing posts and other travelers, weaving in and out of crowds, their warning lights blinking. "I sort of feel like I'm in a parade," whispered Casey.

Brad just smiled and kept his eyes on the luggage. "I don't want anyone to sneak up or add anything to the boxes. Stay alert, dear."

Leaving the building, the handlers stood and watched as Brad and Erick unloaded into the back of the truck until Casey handed them each a tip. They left with alacrity at that point. When the carriers were empty, a security guard told them to just leave the luggage carriers where they were, the men would be back shortly; the public wasn't allowed to take them back inside. He'd call the carriers. Erick closed the tailgate.

"You're right. Squad car would not have held this," he remarked.

"Thanks for coming to get us. We do appreciate it."

"Wouldn't miss it. I need you both back home where we can keep an eye on you. With Founder's Day this weekend, it's going to be all hands on deck. I might even deputize Casey at this point. The crazy festival committee expanded everything to an almost unmanageable size." They got into the truck, Casey choosing to sit in the cab seat in back so the men wouldn't have to talk business over her. She had her eBook reader out and was checking her messages. Erick continued.

"We now have factory tours but the factory people are providing their own security; still, making courtesy calls just in case throughout the day. The barn tour has added two barns so there are an even twelve; five of those have on-site events like hayrides, hay mazes, refreshments, a petting zoo, milking demonstrations, and shearing competitions. In town, they've added a square dance the first evening and a regular dance the second, complete with a loud bluegrass band the first night with a move caller and a disc jockey the second."

"Lord, knows it's going to take us a year to go through the gifts in back and write thank-you notes," started Brad. "And we need to get it done before the weekend. Wish this traffic would let up."

"We get out on Johnstown road and it will. We're still close to the airport."

"Due to the security problems, and the fact people love you both, got to be expected some changes had to be made for safety." began his boss. "Listen. We were going to have the reception at the church when you got back but we agreed that in light of the past kidnappings and attempts on your lives that's just too risky, so I had your mom take the cake and stuff over to your house." Brad considered. "That's probably a good idea. Casey, you OK with not having a big reception in town? We can freeze some of the cake, don't have to eat it all now, and there won't be all the folderol of shaking hands and opening stuff in front of people. It will be fine, right, wife?"

Casey spoke up, "That's fine dear. Mom just texted that she and Annie are waiting at the farm." She got an odd look on her face.

"I thought they were coming out tomorrow?" asked Brad.

"I can't fault them for wanting to see us sooner and oh, dear." She flipped through texts and pictures quickly, her eyes getting larger and larger, more in horror than surprise.

"Might be a little more than that," muttered Erick. He cleared his throat. "I think they brought all the gifts over that were stored at the church so you may have more than what's in back to sort out."

"Well, that makes sense," replied Brad. " We'll have time to get things all settled before I go back to work, it will be fun to see what they all are and if we write thank-you notes as quickly as we unwrap and put in place, yeah, that would be good. Also, I won't have to worry about people getting into the stuff during the festival this weekend. Yeah, that's a good idea, right Casey?" He turned around and got a puzzled expression on his face.

"We'll use what we can but I think we may end up donating the excess to the pantry," replied Casey frowning at the pictures that were being sent to her. "It can help others more than being stored in the closets. I was never much to accumulate a lot."

"Can you believe when we left, she was able to move all her things over from her mom's in just a few trunkloads? Clothes, a few mementos, Annie had more stuff than she did."

"I think we're going to fix that this afternoon," replied the Sheriff. "See, they brought the gifts and the cake and such and I think some folks are planning on welcoming you back."

"How many people are we talking?" asked Brad.

"Well, guys at the station are taking turns coming by, and I think Brent from your office said they'd stop by, you know, your workmates, in the afternoon and I guess your mom and sister and aunt are there, too," started Erick.

"Mom? She hates Rutherford. We were going to pick him up on the way home. Guess I'll need to make a trip in for him."

"He's sort of already there."

"Sort of?"

"Yeah. And some of the Amish have come over with food and it all sort of morphed into a welcome home party." Brad was silent for a minute. He turned around to look at Casey who was still going through texts and looking a little more horrified by the moment.

"Brad, Annie has Rutherford out in the back yard with most the cheerleading squad playing catch. Your mom and sister are sort of sequestered on the front porch, there's a tent over there that must be the food tent, and Annie just sent me- oh wow. Brad, I should have fixed my hair and I really shouldn't be in travel clothes when I get there."

"No time for that," replied Erick. "Have you got a comb she can use?"

"I have a brush in my purse and don't you have to stop for gas? Like right over there immediately, right now, at the Duchess? They have clean bathrooms." Casey sounded like she was taking control. "I have to change clothes and so do you. Brad, you have clean clothes in the suitcase and so do I. I'll meet you out front in ten minutes."

"Casey, you look fine, you really do and I need to get back..." Erick started. Then he saw the look on Casey's face and realized all at once why she was an expert witness for the agency. "Yes, ma'am." He pulled in. They got out and headed for the restrooms while he filled his truck tank. It took less than ten gallons. He cleaned his windshield. He took his time at it, wandered inside to pay for it at the desk instead of using his card, took the longest line, and shortly, Casey came out dressed in her wedding sarong, with a silk flower lei on her hair, which was braided in a waterfall shape. Brad had a matching shirt and shorts. Without a word, they got in and started again to go home.

Chapter Seventeen

Jim went into the room where Troy sat. He was rapidly texting.

"Hi, boss. How are the interviews going?"

"Not badly. I need to ask you the standard stuff and then I need real answers to some bad questions."

After the demographics, Jim studied his clipboard for a few long seconds, then looked up at Troy.

"OK, on to the hard stuff. Troy, I've known you for five years. You've been a good agent, you've come up the ranks, you've got good reviews, you got a promotion coming up. You got a nice family; I've been to your house. Why are you wasting all that with this case?"

"What are you talking about?"

"First, you don't tell us you're related to the suspects and you know that's simply unethical. It will and has gotten you a letter of reprimand which is going to be sent in this afternoon if we don't clear some things up pronto. Second, you didn't mention to me that you'd been in the area last year to do seminars for the local departments six months before the incidents started. You knew who made the blocks, you knew what they most likely represented and you acted all confused like the rest of us instead of being upfront with what you knew. You act like this town is totally new to you, but you lived here, you visited recently, and you knew some of the main people. What is going on?"

"I wasn't upfront because I wanted to know who was using my mother. Yeah, I did have a training trip, I hit several small towns locally, I do trainings; it's part of my job. One of those towns was close to here, I met the sheriff there, like I met a lot of small-town sheriffs at these events. I did drive over and get an updated auditor's map of Lyonsville, but I got them for all the other towns I visited as well. I was not casing the place as you are accusing. I didn't visit my relatives here. None of us have been close since our family broke up; I don't think mom even recognized me when I went over to her place with Erick. It didn't seem pertinent and I didn't put the quilt thing together until I started assembling them in the quilt shop and I wasn't sure so I didn't bring it up. I got the quilt planner board set up and we started putting them together and it dawned on me that those blocks looked like some I'd seen at Marie's but again, I wasn't sure and not going to implicate someone who most likely was innocent. And you're correct in that I should have recused myself but I wanted to catch the nut who was using my mom."

Jim took a piece of paper out of his clipboard and handed it to Troy. "You changed your name from Clamons to Armstrong some years ago after the military when you married. It could be thought that was premeditation for doing all this but how that could possibly be that far in advance, I don't know. I'm going to try and give you the benefit of the doubt. I shouldn't. You've broken several regs and crossed a bunch of lines. You may get drummed out of the force for this and for sure reprimanded if not get jail time. Troy, we've already gone through your schedule to see where you were on the dates of the incidents and you have only got alibis for six out of 23 of them that I can find. I've got the list here. I need you to go through and give me an alibi for every one I can't account for and I want it done in the next half hour. Here's a pad of paper to organize it and remember -- verifiable alibis. I'm going to go talk to Matthew."

Matthew was sitting back in his chair, drinking a soda, playing on his phone, seemingly unconcerned. Jed watched him through the two-way window.

"He doesn't even look worried."

"Anti-socials don't," remarked Jim. "Got my clipboard?"

He traded boards with Jed and went in.

"Morning, Matthew. Sorry you had to wait and we want to get this over with as quickly as possible so first, I need to ask you all the demographic stuff, you know, name, address, that stuff. Then I have some questions about the case we're hoping you might have some answers for."

"What kind of questions?" asked Matthew bringing his chair back up to the table. He had an odd smile on his face. "Is this going to take long? I have customers to see."

"It will take as long as we need to. Now let's have your full name first." Jim went quickly through the list and then asked, "Matthew, you list your address as Chicago. Yet you have an apartment in Columbus with your brothers. No one seems to go there, but you get mail there. Care to explain that?"

"I have an apartment in Columbus for business. I install security systems. I'm good at it. I have a bunch of clients in the Columbus area and I stay overnight there when I'm in town. My other brothers have business there as well."

"They both deny that. They claim they have no idea why their name is on a lease and that they've never paid for it."

"Then they're lying. You ought to have them take one of those lie detector tests."

"Matthew, where is your half-sister?"

"How do I know? She left when I was a kid. Got herself knocked up, Sheila sent her to one of those shepherd homes to adopt out the kid but she never came back home. Last I heard, she was somewhere in Alaska, Alabama, one of the A states."

"When was that?"

"About five years ago. She and her husband move about every five years. She wasn't sure where their next station would be."

"What does she do for a living?"

"I don't know. Never asked. I just get a postcard, that's all."

"Why does she write to you and not the others?"

"She figured one card was all the collective bunch of us were worth. I was supposed to pass it on. She never gave me a return address, it was all just postmarks."

"You have any of those cards?"

"Naw, I didn't keep them. She was nothing to me." Jim looked back to his list of questions and made a note.

"Matthew, how old were you when you went to live with your dad?"

"I was 8." he took a long swig of his soda, crushed the can and tossed it to the wastebasket.

"How long have you worked security?"

"Ten years."

"Same company?"

"I own the company. I started it and it's doing fine. I've got offices in Chicago and Cleveland and setting up one in Columbus."

"Doing well for yourself."

"I got game," nodded Matthew. "You got some more soda?"

"Get you one when I go out from here. Let's see, in the military, you worked munitions?"

"It's called ordnance. Yeah, I blew stuff up."

"Dangerous work."

"It had its moments. Maybe that's why I'm in security now. It's generally quiet."

"There is that," agreed Jim. "You keep in contact with your old teammates?"

"Not so much, just family once in a while. I've been hanging a little with Liam and not as much with Troy. He's pretty straitlaced. Everything by the book, you know. He's really organized."

"That's not a bad thing in an agent."

"If you say so. Liam now, he's tight but he's smart. He knows where to get a bargain, who to talk to to get things done. He's put me in contact with several businesses that needed security and helped me grow the business. He's going to have a baby, he tell you that? I can't wait to be an uncle."

"Yeah, I know. Congratulations. Listen, do you have any kind of contact info on your sister?"

"I told you I didn't."

"Can you tell me if this is your sister?" He showed Matthew a picture of a woman entering the apartment in Columbus. She had turned around to pick up something and her face was caught full-on. Matt sat up.

"What's she doing at our apartment?"

"Matthew, that's the preacher's wife, Lizbeth Primo. She has a key. Watch the security video." The woman went inside for a minute or two and came out with two packages, locked the door and left.

"What is the preacher's wife doing at your apartment picking up packages, Matthew?"

"I don't know. She lives here and so does Liam. Maybe he sent her in for him?"

"What were in the packages, Matthew?"

"I don't know."

"Let's go back and stop the video right, here. That package looks like the one Toby sent to the buyer of his mom's quilt squares. See, we marked the last few packages. See that stamp on the side? That was the mark. Why'd Lizbeth go in and get the quilt blocks, Matthew?"

"How should I know? I didn't even know she was in town."

"She's lived here for four years. She and her husband came four years ago to pastor the church. She has no reason to be involved in the quilt blocks and the crimes. What would be her motive?"

She had to be given the key by one of you three. You just said Troy was a straight shooter; Liam has no reason to get in trouble, who gave her the key?"

"I don't know. It wasn't me. I have mine right here on my key ring."

"Could be a copy."

"She'd have to get one of our three keys to copy. My key doesn't leave my keyring." Jim looked at Matthew for a couple of seconds then reached inside his case and pulled out a list of dates. "You've got your phone with you. I want you to tell me where you were at these times on these dates. In short, I need your list of alibis. I'll go get your soda and compare notes with the other guys."

"Sounds like I may need a lawyer now." glared Matthew.

"That's fine, you call him, too, but you'd best give me traceable alibis or you'll be talking to him from jail."

Jim stalked out, waited three minutes, brought in a soda, and left without comment.

Alli was waiting on him.

"You think he's got alibis?"

"I sure hope not. And we're going to have to talk to the preacher's wife. She shows up on those security tapes several times as picking up packages. And the teacher came out of her coma. Erick's in Columbus picking up Brad and interviewing her."

"She may be our only eyewitness."

"It's possible. Let's hope she remembers."

Chapter Eighteen

Erick drove his pickup into Brad's yard. The porch was full of people, they spilled out of the house, they wandered around from the back. Brad groaned.

"Oh, wow! This was supposed to be a quiet homecoming!" Casey patted his shoulder.

"We can do this, honey," she said. "Let's find the cake and cut it, feed them all, shoo them home with the excuse we have jet lag."

"That could work," replied Erick. "Most folks mean well."

"Oh, they mean well, but wow! And there's my mom and sister and aunt right on the front porch. Oh, wow." Brad shook his head, rolled his shoulders back, stood up straighter, plastered on a smile, took Casey's hand and they walked over to the porch crowd, who promptly started cheering.

Rutherford came plowing through the crowd and launched himself at them both, efficiently knocking them back against the truck.

"Whoa, down Rutherford, down right now!" ordered Brad. The dog did get down, to his credit but pushed himself up against them to prevent them getting anywhere away from him. He was very insistent.

"Now, look, boy, this is home now. We have to go in," began Brad, petting his dog. "Move aside."

"Does he normally act like that?" asked Erick.

"Not usually," replied Brad. "I suspect he really doesn't like having mom or sis on our property. Never did get along with them."

Casey took a big breath. "I can't say as I disagree. Rutherford, let's get this over with. Good boy." She squared her shoulders plastered on a smile and with Rutherford walking close between the two of them, they made their way into the crowd and the family. Congratulations were offered on all sides as the crowd followed them inside. The cake was set up on the kitchen table.

"Hey, can someone help carry in all the boxes and such from the truck and just, well, stack them over there with all the rest of them and we'll get them unpacked later." Several men went out and brought things in.

"Brad, need to talk to you before I go," started the sheriff. "I need to bring you up to speed."

"Can do that," replied Brad. "After we've gotten cake to everyone," said Casey.

She called out, "Thank you all for coming out and helping bring our things in. What say we all have some cake and share a few memories and then I really need to get to bed. Jet lag from Hawaii is pretty fierce stuff."

"Did you guys get any sleep at all on the islands?" grinned her brother.

"The islands were wonderful and when I figure out where the pictures are, I'll show you all. Now, mom? Oh, there you are. Have we got paper plates and such?"

"Absolutely. And you two need to cut the cake for the photographer."

"Malcom?" asked Brad. "You're here?"

"Sure enough, mate. And I even wore shoes. Quite the pretty place you got here. I might not be able to get your wedding pictures but I can at least make a party album for you." Malcom was dressed in his jeans, sandals, and pocket tee.

"Thanks so much," smiled Casey. They posed for pictures cutting the cake, with the people who would have been their bridesmaids and would have been the matron of honor, and the piles of gifts. They even posed with Rutherford. Then Mrs. Armstrong, Annie, and two other ladies started cutting the cake, pouring the punch out, and serving everyone there. Folks walked around outside, Brad and Casey walked here and there thanking people, hugging folks, getting their pictures taken with first one, then the other.

Brad's mom, Aunt Marge, and Allison had their pictures taken as well.

"Well, she does clean up well," muttered Marge to Allison.

"Love her hair," murmured Allison.

"Yes, it is lovely, and getting matching outfits is darling," they posed and smiled. Mrs. Malcom, Brad's crotchety mother, spoke,

"Bradford has a nice place here. She's pretty, I like her. That's the last I'll hear of it. Now I'm going to find out if they're having champagne." Marge and Allison zipped their lips and went to get more punch.

With promises to see everyone at Founder's Day, posing and smiling and pleading jet lag, they finally started seeing folks leave. Brad's mom and relatives left for the bed and breakfast. It was down to Erick, Casey, and Brad, Mrs. Armstrong, and Annie, finally. Erick came in.

"I found these on the banister out front," he announced holding up a vase of flowers. Brad looked at the card.

"It's from Pastor Primo and his wife," he smiled. "How nice."

Casey frowned. "Hey, can you put those outside in the back? I'm terribly allergic to liatris, those purple blossoms. Pretty but if I don't want to be covered in hives, they have to go out now."

"I'll get them," replied the sheriff. He headed out back. "I'll just set them in the wheelbarrow." He sat them down and noticed a piece of fabric coming out of the back and with a really bad feeling, tugged it out. There was a click and he held a quilt square. He backed off fast, holding the square, and was thrown to the ground as the vase blew up.

Brad and his family ran out back just as he stood up and shook himself to be sure he was in one piece.

"What happened?" demanded Brad helping him up.

Mutely, Erick held up the square.

"Courthouse Steps," announced Mrs. Armstrong. "I made one like it as a child. It was from Mrs. Primo?"

"The card is on the counter. Are you OK, Erick?" asked Jed.

"Uniform needed to be washed anyway. I'm calling in the bomb squad."

"There's blood on your shoulder."

"Wheelbarrow is demolished and might have caught shrapnel from it," he moaned. "Shoulder does sort of hurt. And you have a little crater there in the yard."

In short order, the Feds, police, and an ambulance showed up. The Sheriff was taken to the hospital to have pieces of metal removed from his back and shoulder, under protest. Jim and his men checked out the explosion site, took samples.

"Casey, I'm sorry about this but you're going to either have us open all your gifts, or you're going to have to do it in front of us."

"Really?" she gasped.

"Absolutely."

"Wait a minute. The ones from the airport were checked by port authority. They ought to be safe."

Jim shook his head. "No exceptions."

"Then let's set up an assembly line," said Mrs. Armstrong firmly. "Casey, you have a long white table out there folded up in the garage. Bring it out front-you two men.

You, sir, carry the presents out to us in the front yard. Annie, get the garbage can from the back porch, line it with a black plastic bag for the wrapping paper. Take it out front. Everyone move."

"Casey, change clothes so you don't get that pretty dress dirty."

"Mom, I have a photo album here with addresses. Do we have thank-you notes?"

"Absolutely, and here's my clipboard. Let's get this show on the road."

Casey dashed in and changed to jeans and a sweatshirt. Jim took Brad aside.

"Listen, Erick talked to Mrs. Messimer. She's out of the coma, she's weak but remembers what happened. She was getting the big plastic quilt block decals ready to go out to the farmers when she noticed some were missing. She was making a list of what needed to be replaced and who's farm they had been on when Matthew came in. He asked her what she was doing and she explained and he said something about needing some like those and she told him they belonged to the town. She started to give him the address of the place they ordered them: she'd turned around to write it down for him and she had a cloth over her face that smelled sweet; she struggled to push it away, she felt a hit from behind and that's what she remembers until waking up in the hospital. She also said she remembered a woman's voice behind him but didn't recognize it. The security tapes we got from the apartment show Mrs. Primo and Matthew entering the apartment on different occasions and bringing out packages."

"You mean the preacher's wife?" said Brad. "You're kidding. She's just a quiet little thing, always feeding people, running the poor pantry. How did she get involved?"

"Appears she's a half-sister to Matthew."

"Really?" Brad looked thoughtful "As the preacher's wife, she can go just about anywhere and not be noticed or questioned. They've been here, let's see, four, five years now? Matthew has been building up his business locally for four years; Liam has been here three, Troy was here two years ago and last year. You think we have a family clan gang thing going?"

"Possibly," nodded Jim. He looked over at the table and smiled. "Your mom is quite the organizer-look at the assembly line." On the long eight-foot table, Annie sat at the end addressing thank you notes. Mrs. Armstrong was writing them and keeping track of the lists on her clipboard pad; Casey was carefully opening each gift handed to her by the agent. Each gift was carefully being wanded by another man and two others were carrying them all out in the yard. After unwrapping, being noted, and checked off, they were being sat in three piles behind Casey.

Things she was keeping went inside the house and back to the living room. Things she was donating were going to a second pile; things she wasn't sure about to a third.

"It appears one gift every thirty seconds," said Jim. "I could have used that lady at my wedding reception."

"Casey and her mom, just organized, that's all." Jed drove up in the squad car.

"Well, I was hoping for a piece of cake but appears I'm late; Lordy look at that pile of presents! You ought to get married more often, Brad."

"Once is going to be enough," laughed Brad. "Cake's in the kitchen so's punch, cut yourself what you want."

"I'll do that. What I want to know is how you got the feds to come to help out with the thank you notes?" chuckled Jed. "Seriously.?"

"Someone tried to blow us up." replied Brad, quickly outlining it. Jed's face fell.

"Mrs. Primo? Honestly? I just saw her in town with two more vases in the back of her car. She'd stopped to drop one off for the station and said she was going to give the last one to Mrs. Clamons. Said the old lady loved flowers."

Jim looked at Brad. "Jed, hold the cake. We have to get to the station and we have to get to Marie's, stat." Putting his second in charge of the gift checking, Jim and Jed tore off with their siren and lights, back to town.

Chapter Nineteen

Brad started helping with the carrying in of gifts.

"Guys, I can tote them. That will relieve you two to go back to town and help. I have a feeling they're going to need all hands."

"You think there may be more bombs?"

"I am pretty sure that's going to be the case, and the sooner we can get these unwrapped, checked out and put away, the sooner we can get a night's rest and I think I'm going to go back a day or two early. Erick's hurt, and they'll need me." Casey nodded.

"But Rutherford is staying here with you. Mom, Annie, you better stay here tonight. I know you were going to go back home but really, you better not. Where's Casey's brother?"

"I just called him," said Mrs. Armstrong, finishing off a thank you note and handing it to Annie. "He's coming back out and he says he's bringing his guns for cleaning. I told him that wasn't needed but he said he'll just sit out here on the front porch and clean his guns."

"I have enough armory in my gun case he can clean as well," replied Brad, hauling out two more gifts. "Casey, where are you putting the plants?"

"I've unwrapped the three boxes of plants. Those aren't from Hawaii."

"No, those are from me," replied Mrs. Armstrong. "I gave you starts of all your favorites from the yard." Everyone visibly relaxed. "Sorry to be scary."

"No worries, Mrs. A," replied the Fed next to her. "We just don't want anyone else hurt. This is quite a bunch of gifts. You must have a lot of friends."

"Our little town is the best and they love to make sure newlyweds have everything they need, even when they're older and it's not our first." smiled Casey. "Isn't this quilt pretty? I think it ought to go on Annie's bed. Her room is lilac and just look at these iris appliques. What do you think, Annie?" Annie nodded. She continued to look up addresses for folks on her tablet.

"Annie, you OK?" asked Brad.

Annie looked up quickly, then back down.

"Somebody just tried to kill my mom as soon as she got home and I'm supposed to just sit here and write addresses? I want to do something!" She nearly exploded.

Brad went over and patted her on the back. "You and me both. For now, we have to get this done, so we can get ready for tomorrow. And we will find them. We've got a couple of incredible leads right now. And they will be punished to the full extent of the law."

"Besides," said one of the federal agents. "What we do here is going to make you all safer, and the town safer and while it seems like nothing right now, we're being careful. We're at the point in this case where we get very deliberate, very slow almost, like a cat sneaking up on a mouse; the mouse is in sight, the path is straight and this is going to get wrapped up real soon. Don't worry. Your mom and dad are going to be very safe."

Brad went in and another man and they brought out the last gifts.

"That's everything from the living room. In this box are forty-seven envelopes needing to be unwrapped. Can they just be wanded?"

"Most likely. Let me get the sniffer."

"The what?" asked Mrs. Armstrong.

"Sniffer. It's a specialized wand that scents out bomb chemicals," answered Brad.

"What they won't have to have next!" she declared. "So, child, less than fifty more envelopes to look up and address and then we're done. My cake is wearing off and I could do with a pizza."

"Pizza?" asked Brad. "Yep, supposed to be delivered in, let's see, by 6 and it's five-thirty so let's get this done. Rock that address list, dear."

Chapter Twenty

"Yes?" said Pastor Primo as he answered his door.

"Pastor," asked Jed. "Is Lizbeth here?"

"No, she gives away flowers Mondays from the church service to folks in town. She said she would be late because she has to go into Columbus to get floral supplies. There's a store ion the city she gets cases of oasis and wire and such for the flower ladies. She ought to be back, what time is it, anyway?"

"It's four-thirty."

"She said she'd be here by supper and that's at six. Shall I have her call you?"

"If you would be so kind," answered Jed. "We'll just be on our way."

As they left, Jed's companion asked, "Do you think he was hiding her?"

"No, I don't think he knows what's going on." His cell rang.

"What? OK, we'll head over and do that." He hung up. "Matthew and Lizbeth were picked up by Franklin county as they entered the apartment. They're being held for us and we're going to fetch them back for questioning."

"How did they know to stop them? There' no warrant."

"Apartment was under surveillance. We called and got a warrant so if or when they showed up they'd be picked up."

"I sure hope we're getting to the end of this."

"Yeah. This is going to be one long night.

Chapter Twenty-One

Brad thanked the officers and sent them back to the station, assuring them everything was going to be fine now.

"I'll take all these into the post office and mail them out tomorrow when we go back into town," said Mrs. Armstrong. "But for now, the pizza's here. I want to hear about Hawaii, and we need to freeze the top layer of the wedding cake for your anniversary." Brad checked the boxes as he took them into the kitchen, followed by Rutherford being led by his nose.

"Sis, you sure got a lot of nice gifts." Her brother Matthew was wiping down the table.

"And if those island plants live, I want shoots," declared her mom. They all got cans of soda, took pizza, and went out to the back porch to sit.

"Brad, they going to be deputizing people?"

"Before this is over? Maybe. Crowds are going to be thick on the ground during the festival."

"Then I'll shut the shop and join in," said his new brother in law. "These creeps have done too much damage to our family, much less the town."

"Listen, did the cat mummy get home to Thom?" asked Casey.

"Surely did. He's got it back in the display. He left the decal up in the store and people go in to look at it. he told me it was the best advertising he'd had since the break-in. Lots of traffic in the museum."

"Has everything else been more or less quiet?"

"Well, until the vase bombs, we have federal agents all over. Most people are curious but they aren't panicked. Police department is making itself pretty obvious. The folks setting up for the festival are all people we know, local electricians, carpenters, and such. The flower ladies were pretty safe until today, I think. The yarn ladies have bombed the gazebo as expected. It's actually sort of pretty. They've put a little memorial up for Mrs. Harmony's dog. It has a lilac bush planted on it and a little plaque." Matt chewed for a couple of minutes. "School has added security cameras. Both churches are still meeting regularly but they've gotten the deacons in active shooter training. Bad thing to think we need that in a place of worship." Casey nodded. "I got a couple of messages from folks I work with. They've added bullet-proof glass to the receptionist counter, and we have a metal detector now for the entrance. I have to get my badge updated. The new ones recognize us so we can use the back entrance."

"Man alive, it's like the big city has hit the little town and the interconnection of this Venn diagram is not something I'm enjoying. I want my old town back," declared Brad. "And we will get it back. We're really close."

"But the preacher's wife?" asked Matthew. "How could that happen?"

"I don't know. I understand Alli is going to interview her. She's a forensic psychologist. Let's just say I'm glad she's on our side."

Chapter Twenty-two

The squad car pulled up to the back of the station. The little orange Volkswagen was driven and parked beside it and an officer got out. Erick, Jed and Mike accompanied Matthew and Lizbeth through the back door.

Lizabeth was put in room one and Matthew room two. Jim stood outside.

"Sure glad you weren't hurt bad." Jim nodded as he was joined by Erick.
"Nah, didn't need much, they pulled a couple pieces of metal put of my back, got a couple stitches. My guys coming into pick up the suspects gave me a ride home. Little ouchy, but I'm fine. I've heard Alli is quite the interviewer and been curious about her methods. I can always learn new tricks."

"She's good. I'm going to go lean on Matthew a little bit in a few minutes. I want to watch this awhile and Matthew can just stew a bit."

Lizbeth sat at her table with her head bowed, hands folded, sitting straight as an old southern belle. She was pale and she held an old-time cloth handkerchief that was embroidered in some flower motif. When Alli opened the door and came in, she looked up.

"Hi, I brought you some water. We've got a lot of questions to get through and thought you'd get thirsty." She pulled out the chair opposite Lizbeth and sat down, opening a file.

"Let's see, easy stuff first, I need to get your demographics, you know, name and address, that sort of thing. So, full name first?" She looked up at Lizbeth and gave her a bright smile, hand with pen poised for her answers.

"Rebecca Elizabeth Primo. I live at 2367 Church Street, that's the parsonage behind the church. My phone number is 614-345-1368. I am married to Malachi Primo, the pastor the Faith Methodist Church. I don't work outside the home; I am on a lot of committees in my function as a pastor's wife."

"Whoa, hold just a second while I catch up and fill in all these blanks, let's see, what did we miss...oh, date of birth and social?

"I was born May 17, 1980 in Little Rock, Arkansas. 307-34-5678."

"Great. How long have you made flower arrangements?"

"What?"

"You have been doing arrangements for church and you even dropped off one here at the station. Your floral designs are all over town and they're lovely."

"I took an online course years ago when I became a pastor's wife. I've been doing it for 20 years or so?" She seemed to relax and took a sip of water.

"Well, you do an excellent job. The colors and shapes all blend nicely and the vases are so pretty. How long have you been putting bombs in them?"

"What?" Lizbeth's face went white.

"Bombs, you know, the putty stuff in the bottom that is triggered when you either pull out a quilt square or a certain amount of time goes by? We blew the one's at the station here, and at Brad's and the one at Marie's. The ones at the court house have been retrieved and are being dealt with. I'm pretty convinced your husband didn't know anything about them."
"I didn't do that!"

"You delivered them. And we have you on security footage going in and out of an apartment in Columbus, you and Matthew. We know the quilt blocks bought on line all ended up there and then were used in crimes. You need to explain what is going on. You need to cooperate."

"I want my husband Malachi."

"I can call him after we're finished here. The last three vases have your fingerprints on them and Matthew's. His were in the system. We were able to get yours from the vases still at the church. We removed those also. I don't think you're a naturally horrible person or anything. I just need to understand why you and Matthew are going after a small town. I like to understand motives. It's what I do. Matthew is after revenge. He was pretty upset that you'd taken a vase over to Marie. He didn't know about that one. What was your rationale for trying to kill a little old lady who hasn't done anything to you?"

Lizbeth sat frozen for a few minutes. She shook her head several times. She started to shudder and her face got pale. She started to whisper.

"They wouldn't let me keep my baby," she said softly. "I never had another baby. They took the baby away and wouldn't even let me hold it. I don't know if it was a girl or a boy; I wasn't allowed to know. They took it away."

"Who took it away?" asked Alli. "What baby?"

"And that old lady was the start of it. If she would have just kept that man away from my mother, mom wouldn't have married him, we'd have been fine without him. It's all her fault. If she hadn't been such a prissy, fussy woman, Jack would never have taken up from mom and I'd have never gotten pregnant."

"I still don't understand. Jack left her, not the other way around. He ran off and took the boys."

"Yeah, he did. He took off, he and his blessed boys." she almost shouted. "They all descended on our home. We had a nice house that my dad left us when he died. We were happy. Mom had a good job. Jack was supposed to be my new dad." she snorted and shook her head. "It wasn't very long before he was in my bed as well as mom's. And I got pregnant and when I told my mom she slapped me and called me a whore and she sent me to this shepherd's home place. I stayed there until I had the child and they wouldn't even let me see it; they said it would be easier that way. But I hear her crying in my dreams, I see her in every baby I've seen over the years in churches. When mom and Jack broke up and they sent all those boys here and there, I thought I could come home but mom blamed me. She said I broke up her marriage with my whoring ways. I was seventeen and no place to go. I had completed my high school at the home, and I applied for college and I went. I'm not stupid. I'm not. I just didn't understand the whole thing that happens when a new dad comes in. I didn't know why he wanted to sleep with me the nights mom worked. I'd never been with a man before. I didn't know how to not get pregnant." She drew a deep breath and took a swig of water. "I went to school and I studied to be a CPA. And I passed it. I met Malachi at college. He was going to be a missionary and I figured I'd be so far away I'd never have to see this little town again. We went to Alaska once he was ordained for five years and then Hawaii for five and I made good friends there."

"Friends who would send a package for you?" asked Alli.

Lizbeth nodded. "Friends who would pass on a package to a bridal couple for me. And we went to Washington State and one day Malachi came home and said he had grand news. We were going to Ohio, not far from where I grew up, and I'd be able to reconnect with my family and old friends. He had no idea I'd had a child. He didn't know Jack had gifted me with an STD and I couldn't have any more kids. I had several miscarriages. I thought the move would be OK, I mean, it's twenty years later. It hurt driving past our old home and seeing other people living there, but that's in another town; here was just Marie's place, and it looks different after twenty years and she didn't even own it. Everything was fine until I saw Liam and then Marie went to our church. Neither of them recognized me. I used to have long hair, and wear jeans, lots of make-up and I talked trash. I dress like a proper pastor's wife now. I dress prissy like Marie used to so before she had to go work in the paint factory. But Matthew figured out who I was. He was still angry about everything. He said we needed to show this town just what they'd done when they drove Jack out and into me and mom's lives. I didn't know he was going to get so violent. I was stunned by the library explosion." She looked at Alli as if seeing her for the first time. "Why wouldn't they let me hold my baby? Just a minute or two? Just to have it in my arms, just a few minutes. The baby won't stop crying."

She held up her arms as if she'd just seen them. "But they said mom had signed papers saying it was to be adopted out and back then, I was a minor, I had no rights. Those nuns told me to just think of it as a gift given to God and not worry, they'd see it had a good home. They called my baby it; I wasn't allowed to know it' sex. When I'd had my six weeks check -up I was supposed to go home. Mom would let me come back." she shook her head and drew in a breath. "I didn't know about what was in the vases. Matthew asked me about the flowers I always delivered." Alli just kept nodding, making small noises and letting Lizbeth talk. She reached over and patted Lizbeth's hand. She'd aid down her notes and file and just watched Lizbeth.

"I never really wanted to hurt anyone but Matthew said we needed to show them how much they'd hurt us. When he talked about getting back, I thought he was going to, I didn't know, break some windows? Spray some graffiti? He took pictures of all the places he planned to attack and he kept it on a laptop. I got desperate about that laptop and I told Liam about it. E had to know what he was going to do next. Matthew threatened Liam to get him to kidnap the deputy's wife. He told him all he had to do was get them in the car and put them to sleep. He wasn't going to hurt them, just scare them a little. If Liam didn't do it, he was going to tell Liam's wife about everything. Matthew had enough on everyone to blackmail them into going along. Matthew had it all on that laptop and if we had it, then his plans would fall through. Or at least we'd know what to expect and be able to warn people. Liam sneaked it out of Matthew's car and he put it in the church for me. I went to get it but the police were there and there was a body on the pulpit. My poor Malachi was terribly upset over it. So was I." She took a long drink of water before continuing. She rubbed her temples.

"I'm getting one of my headaches. My head hurts so bad and I can't hear anything but the baby crying."

"How did you decide to put the quilt blocks everywhere?" asked Alli as she also mirrored Lizbeth's actions, rubbing her temples and taking a drink. She folded her arms around her, as Lizbeth had done and then after a few seconds, she opened them up and laid them on the table within easy reach.

"I don't know, I don't remember which one of us thought about the quilt squares, I guess when Toby told Liam about selling them on line for his mom, Matthew heard about it, went to the site and started buying them. He said we'd frame the woman who made me hurt so bad. It was before we'd done anything. And then it all just got out of hand. He told me he used to dream about it when he was in the military, how he'd put her in jail. He got that apartment and put all their names on the lease so if he got implicated, they would too; if they wouldn't help him, he could blackmail them. He didn't put Toby's name on it; he calls him the family idiot. Liam he black mailed into taking Casey and her mom out of town, but Matthew met him and Liam went home. He got Liam to get him some chemicals for experiments: I'm pretty sure Liam didn't know what they were for. Toby never knew his part in selling the blocks on line. It was like they were all of them in it and one of them knew it, you know? God! It feels good to talk about it! It's all so out of control." she paused. "May I get my inhaler out of my purse? They took my inhaler. It sometimes helps." Alli called out and asked that the purse be brought to her. She knew it had already been searched and there were no weapons and there was an asthma inhaler in it and some other medicines. The police had called the doctor and verified they were Lizbeth's. An officer brought the inhaler in and handed it to Alli who gave it to Lizbeth who took a sniff of it. She waited a second and then started again.

"Matthew enjoys hurting people. I just thought we were going to scare people a little, make them remember what they'd done here to us all. I never thought he'd hurt anyone. I actually helped him think of some of the stuff like putting the lines on the buildings in quilting patterns. I didn't realize he'd killed anyone or kidnapped anyone until later and when I tried to talk to him about it, he threatened to pin it on Malachi. My poor Malachi. He's good man. He's a little dense about some stuff, and really naive. He's a good man. He's going to be so hurt when he realizes what kind of a person he's been married to all these years." She paused and handed the inhaler back to Alli who took it and set it behind her for safety. "You don't have to worry. I'm not suicidal or homicidal or anything. I'm pretty calm. I deserve jail. I hope they can lock me up and that it really is so loud all the time I won't hear the baby anymore. I wish I could stop her crying." She took a breath. "Once Matthew started getting more violent and threatening me, I tried to back away; I even told Malachi we needed to look for another parish. He doesn't want to. I couldn't tell him why. If they had just let me hold my baby: I keep hearing the cry: I heard it cry when it was born and that's all I can hear some nights when I wake up. I hear the baby cry. It's out there somewhere and it never knew me. My arms feel so empty. It's why I can't do baby showers. Malachi thinks it's because of my miscarriages but he doesn't know. I can't hold a baby. I wouldn't be able to let it go." Her voice broke and she began to sob.

Outside the room, Jim looked at Erick. "I think that's my cue to go talk to Matthew. Alli's recording this. I feel for her husband."

"I think she just snapped. I am not sure at all she knew what she was doing." said Erick softly.

"You may be right. It won't bring back the dead. She needs help. What a life."

Chapter Twenty-three

Matthew listened to Lizbeth's confession with a stoic face and demanded his lawyer. Jim read him his rights in front of the lawyer he'd called in, and played the video back for them both. Matthew, after his initial anger, and consulting with the lawyer, agreed to give them some information, but saved most of it for negotiations.

"Negotiations?" asked Jim.

"Yeah, you want to know where the bodies are buried, then you offer me something in return. I know how this goes." he snarled.

"Matthew, don't say another word. We need to discuss how defense."

Jim spoke quietly. "Unless he tells me immediately if and where nay other bombs are planted, I am leaving this room and looking him for 4 first degree murders, willful destruction of property, domestic terrorism and several other charges. He will be lucky to get off with the death penalty. "I need to confer with my client," said the lawyer quietly.

"You have five minutes." he slid a tablet and pen across the table.

"I want list of all remaining bombs and possible problems. I will send men to check those sites and if they turn out to be good information, and nothing else happens, I'll confer with our legal people and see what charges we have to file and which can be amended. Five minutes." Jim got up and left the room. He had Erick watch the discussion and he made a call to the Prosecutor. He'd earlier sent the confession over. She was busily setting up charges for each family member.

"I don't think Toby is going to be charged with anything. He did nothing but try and help his mother." The Prosecutor said. "Liam, it could be argued, was blackmailed under duress and threat. The right lawyer could get his charge of kidnapping thrown out: he was told they wouldn't be harmed but his wife would be if he didn't help, so as long as he cooperates with us, charges will be dropped. We will do a kidnapping charge and accessory to crime, but expect full cooperation and they'll be dropped. Lizbeth, it can be argued has a mental health defense, but for sure accessory to crime fits. We'll most likely settle with her going into in house therapy for a couple years and some sort of restitution. Matthew, it could also be argued, has a mental health defense based on his PTSD and such, but he has shown a lot of premeditation, so kidnapping, murder, domestic terrorism, theft, larceny, assault, he might not get the death penalty but he's not seeing the light of day for years. See what you can get but this is going to be one heck of a plea bargain to work out. Troy's career just took a dive. He's going to be lucky to be reassigned to Siberia."

After the call, Jim reentered the room. The lawyer was writing and stopped as he entered.

"I have a proposal here agreed upon by my client. In exchange for a dropping of the murder 1 charges, he will give you the location of the remaining bombs, of which there are three. They are paced to go off one a day during the Founder's Day festivities and set to cause the maximum damage. His intent was to totally destroy the town." The lawyer looked a little green as he drew a breath. "And after this, I am going to petition the court to appoint him a federal lawyer as I am not qualified to hear Domestic terrorism cases. I'm not qualified to prepare a defense for federal court. I assume this is going that way?"

"What?" demanded Matthew.

"You need a lot more qualified lawyer than I am. When you started bombing things and Homeland got involved, and when you kidnapped people, it became a federal case. You're going to need a lot more than me to get out of that." He turned to Jim.

"Do we have a deal?"

"We can drop the accidental death of the infant and older lady from the bombing to involuntary manslaughter. The deliberate murder of Mr. Drummel and Mr. Dickson, showing premeditation, are staying at murder one. We might be able to drop the demand for the death penalty. That is as good as it's going to get."

The lawyer drew a deep breath and looked at Matthew. "Matthew, I cannot impress on you the necessity of cooperation at this moment. It's time to stop the revenge and actually start pulling back from all this. What you do over the next five minutes are going to show whether or not you're going to get out of this alive. My advice is to accept what they're offering in return for information. It's the best you're going to get and if something else does blow, there is no way you come back from it."

Matthew defiantly looked form one to another man, then shook his head. "OK, write it up. I am not making a confession at this point. There is a bomb in the records department at the court house. There's one under the gazebo in the park. There are three under and in the paint factory."

"Where are those located exactly?" asked Jim, writing.

"One's in the chemicals room, where they keep the solvents and such. Ones in the general manager's office in the desk. Last one is in the main security system box that's attached to the electrical box."

"We'll dispatch men to those sites and find them. Once this information is verified, I'll get the prosecutor to get the list of charges to you based on what we know now instead of tomorrow. It might shorten the list for you. Counsel, you maybe need to make up a list of acceptable federal lawyers."

The information was good; the bombs were found and eliminated. The squad went over each and every original place of business looking for more right up until the Friday of Founder's Day.

Founder's Day weekend dawned bright and pretty. The entire town showed up and the temporary parking places by the school for the buses bringing in tourists and the extra cars did a booming business. The houses had been trimmed by their owners in preparation for the contests. Judges with large ribbons pinned to their shirts walked around judging everything in sight. The list of things you could win prizes from grew from three to fifteen.

Over by the gazebo, the mayor got up to make his speech and was interrupted by a huge woof and a bevy of middle school cheerleaders bounced up, cartwheeling and rolling, flipping and shouting. They made a chorus line in front of the gazebo and began to chant:

"Hey Hey, What do ya say?

We're all here for Founder's Day!

Hey, HO

What do you know?

Nothing else is going to blow.

Hey, Hi

What do we try?

Gonna tell the blues good bye!"

At this line, Rutherford dashed over to the squad carrying a basket of flags. The girls grabbed the basket and dashed through the crowd, handed them to everyone who quickly got into the spirt of things and waved their flags enthusiastically.

The Mayor finally got to start his speech.

In the back of the crowd, an older lady n a wheelchair sat watching the proceedings with an armload of flowers in her lap. Toby and Marie enjoyed their day. He bought her a banana split from a vendor and hot fudge sundae for himself. Brad and Casey walked through the crowd, Brad on duty so they didn't hold hands but did manage to steal a few kisses here and there.

"Well, darling, the Federal agents have all gone home. The office is quiet. The crime wave is stopped. And except for the yarn bombings, the town is almost back to normal."

"We'll get through Founder's weekend, and you are still going to square dance with me! And we can just go home in peace and quiet. How are all the other Clamons?"

"Liam and Troy turned state's evidence. Troy gave a deposition and was reassigned to I'm guessing Timbuktu. Liam gave evidence and plea bargained any charges down to misdemeanors that won't leave us without a pharmacist. Marti is adding to the house and there's a chance she's adding a large doghouse for Liam to live in for the immediate future. I understand Melissa is going to retire from teaching soon. She's been trying for five years. Marie has maybe a few more weeks to live, but don't know. She is a tough old girl. She might fool them yet. Look at her eating ice cream."

Casey ran up. "Mom! Hold my pom-pom. The squads going for snacks and then we're going shopping and David said I could ride his horse."

"David?"

"Yes! The Amish are giving buggy rides."

"Go change out of the uniform first."

"Yeah, we're all changing over at the Fiber Avalanche. She's got the best snacks!" Casey chased off.

"You going to be holding pompoms all day?"

"No, I'll stick them in the car."

"Well, Mrs. Malcom. Seems to me we need to scurry over there and come back."

"I need protected to go put stuff in the car?" she grinned at him.

"Maybe not so much protected as doing a lot of accompanied..." he smiled back. To the sound of the high school band, they strolled through the crowds, talked to neighbors and thoroughly enjoyed a mostly calm Founder's Day.

Thank you for reading the first mystery trilogy of Fiber Maven Mysteries, there are several more to follow. This one dealt with quilts, the next one will follow Brad and Casey as they unravel a mess of knotted rovings. You can follow us on our author page on Amazon, or our webpage or FB to find out when the next mystery comes out. I can give you a couple hints: spinning, alpaca, dye pots and toddlers.

But in the meantime, as we complete the editing and design for the next book, if you enjoy Christian fiction, you might enjoy the series I completed last year called The Oberllyn Family Chronicles. It traces the stories of a single family through three centuries in America, past, preset times and future, with an eye on warning all those of us who love liberty and love the Lord what could happen to our freedoms if we don't guard them and pay attention to what is happening. The first book in the Series, <u>The Oberllyn's Overland</u>, deals with the family at the time of the Civil war and the Western Expansion. *Here's the first couple chapters:*

"Well, mother, it's just about all I can stand," remarked Elijah Oberllyn as he stepped into the kitchen.

"What happened this time?" answered his wife Elizabeth. She was busy rolling out the dough for homemade noodles on the wooden kitchen table. Behind her on the woodstove was bubbling a rich broth to cook them in. From the oven came the wonderful smell of peach pie baking, and warm bread stood on the counter, covered in tea towels. Elizabeth was short woman, with her long black hair, just starting to show grey, done up in a bun at the back of her neck, wearing a solid brown apron over a calico brown dress, and she looked capable of taking on the entire army and feeding it at once. Bustling as she rolled out the dough, she reminded you of a wren on a branch, swaying and hopping from task to task, chirping merrily in between.

"That neighbor Jacks," began her husband. "He's let his cattle get into my wheat again. He says he'll mend the fence but this time he said it was my fault because if I hadn't planted wheat, his cows wouldn't have been tempted, and he is talking about suing me for tempting his cows!"

His wife looked at him and finally said, "You're serious? He is going to try suing you for tempting cows?" She started to laugh out loud but hushed herself when she saw how angry her husband was. "It appears to me the only person to benefit from that would be the lawyers."

"He wants my field to add to his farm. He won't mend the fences on purpose. He's expecting me to do his fence. He's doing the same thing to our son. He offered him a pittance for his orchard, and when Noah wouldn't sell, he started rumors about him being half crazed since the church kicked him out during the great Disappointment and not being right so some of our own neighbors are questioning us for having our own services and I simply am not sure what to do. It's bad enough he picks on us but really, taking off after my son is just about all I can stand." Elizabeth considered for a moment, then said quietly to her husband,

"It's not much of a witness to be fighting with the neighbors. Joe wants to go to California to hunt for gold, but Catherine is not about to drop everything for a wild goose chase. Noah seems content here. I haven't spoken to Mary or Emily about it. I suppose we could consider moving but I hate the idea."

"We've lived here peaceably with our neighbors for years. It's only since those Jacks moved into their uncle's farm we've had trouble. Our land is fertile enough, but when Jacks heard we'd tried to buy his uncle's farm once, he took a dislike to us. And now look." Her husband poured himself a cup of coffee and sat down, blowing on it to cool it, then looking at is wife with a pensive expression on his face.

"California is a right far piece to go," he started.

"Elijah! I was only giving you ideas from different members of the family, not saying I wanted to go." His wife turned with her hands on her hips, a distinctly displeased look on her face.

"It's a good idea and I might have to look into it. I don't want to be run out of town on a rail and that's just what that Jack's fellow is going to try and make happen. Besides, it's getting too crowded around here. It wasn't so bad before that train got put in. Now there are more people coming to buy land and settle in and it's just too crowded."

"Well, you need to pray about anything before you go off half-cocked," she said firmly. "Now go do your chores whilst I finish up supper."

Elijah went back to his barn and finished cleaning out stalls. His wife's jerseys would be up soon for milking. They'd cost him a pretty penny when he'd gotten them, but had proven to be just what Ma's dairy business needed. They gave rich milk, it made wonderful cheese and butter, and their farm was getting known for its good fruit and cheese. Until that neighbor had moved here, everything had been going along fine. Joe had a good thought, though. Out west, there was plenty of land and it wasn't crowded. They could worship as they pleased on Saturday and not be accused of being Judaizers or crazy or anything else. He had two more children at home and there'd be no land to give them as a farm of their own if he couldn't buy up some land. When his son Nathaniel got married, it was a good thing he was a doctor who hadn't time to farm. The farm was just too divided up as it was, what with Emily and her brood, and Catherine and David over by the creek running the small fruits part of the family business. Miriam's man Joe being a lawyer had helped; they'd just needed land for a house and little garden for themselves, no real farming involved. Noah and Mary had taken over the fruit orchard and were making a good go of it, and he and Elizabeth still had enough for him to raise the best horses and oxen in the county and keep mom's dairy running, but they needed more land. It just couldn't be divided anymore and there was Thomas and Johanna yet to be grown and have a part. He supposed Thomas could inherit their home but where would Joanna go? And that Jacks trying to force them to sell land to him they didn't have to spare, he and his dirty tricks. Hard to imagine what he'd try next. Maybe Joe had a good idea. *I believe I'll just visit the land office and find out about land west of here. It surely wouldn't be bad to have a look.*

He came out of the barn and stretched. His son Thomas came dashing up; that child never went anywhere at a walk, always running. "Pa, you got a letter."

"Oh? Thank you, son. Let's have a look." He took the letter from him. It was an official looking document from the US government.

"Haven't seen one of these since well before you were born."

"Was that back when you and mama lived in New York?"

"Yes, pretty much when you were a baby, before grandpa died and we inherited the farm."

"Wonder what they want?"

"Whatever it is, your mom and I will deal with it. You're supposed to have seen to the goats."

"Done. You know the mom angora is going to give birth any day?" he grinned. "Can't wait to see them. I love the way the babies sprong around."

"Well, you keep a good eye on her."

Thomas hesitated. "Pa, I saw Mike Jacks over looking at mom's sheep. He had this funny look on his face?"

"Funny like how?"

"He said his dad doesn't like sheep, they ruin the field. I told him it wasn't his field so not to worry about it. He said something under his breath and walked off. I don't like him much, pa. I was hoping for a friend that would move in that I could do stuff with but I don't think he likes me much."

"Don't worry about him. There are other folks to be with that don't cause such aggravation. Just be civil and leave him be."

"Yes, pa. He made Johanna cry. Oh!" he covered his mouth.

"What?"

"I wasn't supposed to tell you."

"Stop right now. You don't keep secrets from me, ever. When was Johanna crying?"

"She went out to get the cows yesterday and Ellie Jacks was waiting and called her a cowgirl and teased her about her hair."
"What's wrong with her hair?"

"It's sort of red, I guess. And Johanna was crying when she helped with milking."

"I see. And you weren't supposed to tell me?"

"Johanna said we were having enough trouble with this family and God wouldn't want her complaining about it."

"I see. Well, you just let me handle this. Must be about time for supper, yes, there's mom ringing the dinner bell. Let's go wash up."

Dad and Thomas washed up at the pump and went inside, hanging their hats by the door.

"That smell sure chirks a fellow up, ma. Can't wait to have some of your chicken and noodles." Elizabeth smiled.

"Johanna, would you mind getting the field tea I made? I put it in the springhouse to get cold." Johanna nodded and went out the door, coming back with a pitcher covered in a towel.

"Mom," she frowned. "I don't think we ought to use the tea."

"What's the matter?"

"Somebody's been in the spring house."

"Really? How do you know?"
"The cheese's are all on the floor and the milk's spilt." Ma and Pa rushed outside to the spring house where they found rounds of cheese scattered all over, the five-gallon milk cans flipped, polluting the spring run over. They looked around at the damage. Ma shook her head.

"I hate to think we'd have to put guards on our home, but this is outrageous."

"If we tell the sheriff," began Thomas.

"He'll say it could've been done by animals, that someone left the door open. There's no proof."

"Why don't we make a list of what's going on at least and ask him to watch out with us?" asked Ma.

"We can do that. Are the cheeses ruined?"

"The shelves are broken down, but the cheese ought to be fine. I may have to rewrap some.."

"Let's see what we can do. Thomas - call Mick and Mike." Mike and Mick were the family mastiffs who spent most the time in the back field with the cattle. The dogs came to Thomas's call. "We'd best keep the dogs close to the yard or at least one of them here."

"Then who's going to protect the cattle from coyotes?" asked Thomas.

"It's not the four-legged ones I am worried about just now."
Thomas and dad reset the shelves, and they helped mom wipe off the wax coated cheeses and set them back. While they did that, mom set the milk cans up and opened the overflow wide so the water could drain out and run clear. Finally, they stood up and went out. Dad shut the door to the spring house and set Mike by the door, telling him to stay. He took Mick to the barn and set him there and they went inside to eat.

The meal was a quiet one. Ma and Pa were tight-lipped and Thomas and Johanna were quiet as they passed food around.

"I don't care what they say. Johanna, you have got the prettiest hair in the world. It shines in the sun like gold and when you wear your green Sabbath dress I have the prettiest sister in the county."

Johanna looked surprised and her eyes welled up. "Thank you," she whispered.

"I agree with your brother. I am not quite sure why he said it but thank you for noticing," said Pa. Mom and Johanna just looked confused. Suddenly, there was a loud meow from out back.

"What on earth!" said Ma, getting up. She went out back where a strange collie dog had her pet cat up a tree. She took a switch and chased it off. The dog ran to the end of the driveway where Mike Jacks was watching.

"Lady, you'd better not hurt my dog," he yelled at her.

"Then keep him on your own land," she replied.

"Well, this is going to be our land when my dad gets done with you," he yelled back. "You'd better not let those sheep overgraze it." Mom picked up a bigger switch and headed down the drive purposefully in his direction and he ran off. A passing wagon stopped.

"You all right, Mrs. Oberllyn?" said the farmer driving.

"I don't know, Zeb. We got neighbor problems. My spring house was attacked, they insult us and we just never did them any harm."

"I heard about some of that. Mr. Jacks was in the general store last week boasting he'd have your land soon. I don't know what he was talking about but I was coming to tell your husband if he was going to sell out, to call on me. I could use good fields like yours."

"I thank you, and I'll tell Elijah, but we have no interest in leaving our farm. It's been in the family for over a hundred years."

"Thought he might be blowing smoke. But still, keep me and my sons in mind. I'd rather buy from you than Jacks. Oh, and best be careful. Theres some weird rumors going around." Elijah was on the porch and waved to his neighbor.
"Rumors?"

"I'm sure they ain't true. You say howdy to Elijah for me."
"Thank you, Zeb. By the way, did he happen to say why he wanted my land?"
"He said it was the best land in the district and I have to agree with him. Your orchards make the best fruit, your cheese is wonderful and you've always been real supportive of our community. Shame to have you leave."

"Aren't planning on leaving.."

"I hope not. Well, I best be getting home. You remember my offer."

Mom went to the back where Thomas had climbed the tree and gotten her Maine coon cat down. He jumped into her arms. "There, there, dear. I'm sorry he flustered you so. Shh, now. Shhh."

"Mom, why do they hate us?"

"I have no idea." They went inside. "We've never had this much trouble."

"Mom, did you know Jacks have got slaves?"

"What?"

"They have three of them. I saw them out working his field. And Mr. Jacks carries a whip."

"I see. Well, the good Lord never wanted slavery. We earn our needs by the works of our hands, not the sweat of others. Let's try to finish supper. It's most likely all cold by now."

About the Author:

J. Traveler Pelton was born in West Virginia in the last century. She served as Nation's Mother for her tribe, for six years. She is wife to Dan (45 years!), mother of six adults, a grandmother of eight, a Clinically Licensed Independent Social Worker with Supervisory Status, at present in private practice, a retired adjunct professor of social work at her local university and an insatiable reader. She is a cancer survivor. Traveler avidly studies science and technology, fascinated by the inventiveness of people. She is quick to draw parallels in different fields and weave stories around them. Traveler is a fabric artist and her most enjoyable time is spent spinning yarn while spinning yarns for the grandkids.

You can reach Traveler at her website:
travelerpelton.com

Or like us and share us on **Facebook at Traveler Pelton**
Or write to her by **snail mail** at

Springhaven Croft
212 Sychar Rd.
Mt. Vernon, OH 43050

She loves to hear from her readers!

All our books are available on Amazon as both eBook and print copy, Kindle unlimited as free downloads

We'd love it if you'd leave us a review! It helps others find our books.

God bless and see you in our next travels together!

Your Attention Please!!!!

Would you like to join the team at Potpourri Books?

Traveler is always looking for responsible beta readers
for her new books. A beta reader gets a prepublication copy
of all new books, free of charge in exchange for an honest
review written on Amazon, and a short email letting her know
of any glitches you may have found that got past the editor,
any suggestions you may have, and your opinion of the book.
What else do you get out of it?

A beta reader gets:
A free download of one of her already published books
and
as soon as your review of that book gets placed on
Amazon,
free downloads of her already published works: for each
review, you get a free book.
And
A free copy pre publication copy of all new books…
And
Other neat freebies as they come, from bookmarks to
stickers to posters to pens to neat things I find to send out to
my betas-
Interested?
Contact Traveler at
travelerpelton@gmail.com for more info…

We would love to add you to the team!

Dear Lord,
Give me a few friends
who will love me for what I am,
and keep ever burning
before my vagrant steps
the kindly light of hope...
And though I come not within sight
of the castle of my dreams,
teach me to be thankful for life,
and for time's olden memories
that are good and sweet.
And may the evening's twilight
find me gentle still.

Old Celtic blessing....

I've seen better days, but I've also seen worse.
I don't have everything that I want, but I do have all I need.
I woke up with some aches and pains, but I woke up.
My life may not be perfect, but I am blessed."
Anonymous

Until you join me on another journey, may you be blessed as well!

www.ingramcontent.com/pod-product-compliance
Lightning Source LLC
Chambersburg PA
CBHW031304160726
47993CB00001B/299